"I marry J...
The whispered...
"I can't leave my island. It's all Samson and I have left. It's our home."

"Then you agree to the marriage?"

She thought hard, but no better solution came to her. "Yes, Uncle Edward. Prepare the way for my wedding. I guess I'll marry the outlaw."

"You'll marry a gentleman. I'll have you see it no other way."

"Perhaps you should reintroduce me to my groom."

PAIGE WINSHIP DOOLY is the author of over a dozen books and novellas, with four more books due out in the next year. She enjoys living in the coastal Deep South with her family, after having grown up in the sometimes extremely cold Midwest. She is happily married to her high school sweetheart and loves their life of adventure in a full house with six homeschooled children, a cat, and three dogs.

Books by Paige Winship Dooly

HEARTSONG PRESENTS
HP84—Heart's Desire
HP775—Treasure in the Hills
HP807—The Greatest Find
HP820—Carousel Dreams
HP840—The Petticoat Doctor

The Lightkeeper's Daughter

Paige Winship Dooly

Heartsong Presents

A note from the Author:
I love to hear from my readers! You may correspond with me by writing:

Paige Winship Dooly
Author Relations
PO Box 721
Uhrichsville, OH 44683

ISBN 978-1-60260-883-2

THE LIGHTKEEPER'S DAUGHTER

All scripture quotations are taken from the King James Version of the Bible.

All of the characters and events in this book are fictitious. Any resemblance to actual persons, living or dead, or to actual events is purely coincidental.

Our mission is to publish and distribute inspirational products offering exceptional value and biblical encouragement to the masses.

PRINTED IN THE U.S.A.

one

Little Cumberland Island, Georgia, 1867

"I know Papa's coming back, Samson. Don't try to tell me otherwise."

Hollan climbed to the top of the largest sand dune with Samson following close at her side. As they neared the peak, he nudged past her and plopped onto the sand. She sank down beside him. Her stamina wasn't keeping up with the rapid improvements in her vision. They'd searched for her father as far as she dared. With her eyesight coming and going, she was afraid to go too far. "We just need to find him, that's all."

Samson released a small whine.

"With Mama it was different. I knew she was gone. My heart knew. But this time, with Papa—" She stopped a moment and gave her next words some thought, then shrugged. "I don't know. With him, it's different. He's out there somewhere. I'm sure of it. We just need to figure out where. It's only been a day."

Samson lifted his furry head and raised an eyebrow.

"You think I'm crazy, don't you, boy?" She reached over and ruffled his tawny fur before settling on her back beside him.

The cloudless blue sky overhead stretched in all directions. The gentle breeze blew in off the water, carrying with it the salty scent of the ocean. Hollan inhaled deeply.

Her vision had steadily improved during the past few months, going from nothing but blurred shapes, as it had been for most of the past three years, to dim but specific outlines of objects and people. She hadn't told her father about the improvements, not wanting to get his hopes up if the experience was fleeting, but every day brought her more clarity.

Until now. . . . This moment brought her colors and clarity and. . .

"Samson!" She shot to an upright position and looked around.

Samson raised his head and barked, alert for pending danger. When he didn't see any, he looked at her in confusion.

"I *saw* your eyebrow quirk! I can see you staring at me like I've finally lost my mind. I can see the sky and the water and—oh Samson! I can see it all!"

The ocean-side view spread before them. Hollan could see every detail clearly: the sea oats, the waterline, the birds, a faraway boat on the horizon.

"Samson, I can see the water." Hollan held her breath, afraid that if she moved wrong or breathed too deeply the vivid scene in front of her would melt away. "Not only can I hear the waves, I can see them."

The sun played across the water, causing it to sparkle. A fin cut through the surface, though from this distance Hollan couldn't tell if it belonged to a dolphin or a shark. The movement—straight up, then forward for a few feet, then straight down—more closely resembled that of a shark. Dolphins tended to move in arched patterns, rolling up over the surface and back down, and they usually appeared and disappeared over and over until they moved out of view. She longed to see a dolphin. It had been too long.

Samson didn't respond other than to stare. She leaned down and peered into his dark brown eyes. She hadn't looked into a set of eyes in more than three years, and Samson's doggy eyes were just beautiful. It was a perfect moment. Samson reacted to the direct contact by wagging his tail.

"I know, Sam. This is a gift. It's precious."

Her vision blurred, and she panicked, wiping quickly at her eyes. She stared down at her hands. Tears. She could see the crystal clear liquid on her fingers. Her vision wasn't receding. The tears caused the blur.

"If only I could see Papa, Sam." She looked into her dog's eyes again. "He'll come home soon, right?"

Samson laid his head on his paws and stared out over the water.

Dark storm clouds appeared on the horizon.

"The next storm is already on its way, boy. I guess we aren't going to get a break in the weather for as long as I'd hoped."

Hollan wanted to savor the view, but she knew with her vision coming and going she needed to do some chores while she was still able.

⋅≈⋅

"Maybe he's not coming back." Hollan whispered aloud the words her heart had wondered about for the past three days. Words she hadn't wanted to voice because stating them might make them real. Each passing day caused her more concern. Her father had never left her, not even for a day, and there was no way he'd leave her now unless he had no choice. Had she lost him to the most recent violent storm? She'd lost her mother during a similar squall three years earlier. She pushed back her panic and forced herself to take a few deep breaths. Perhaps he'd only been hurt. But deep down she knew even if he'd been hurt, he would have found a way to get back to her. Just as he always had in the past.

She squeezed her eyes shut against the thought, warding off the image of her injured father needing her when she was unable to find him. The reality that she'd kept pressed against the back of her mind insisted on forcing its way forward. If her father had been injured enough not to make it back, surely he wouldn't be alive three days later. Their part of the island wasn't that big.

Hollan faced the ocean and listened to the harsh waves as they crashed against the sandy shore—the sound the last remnant of the most recent destructive storm. The beach would be scattered with debris—driftwood, seaweed, and other odds and ends that always washed ashore with the waves.

But she wouldn't know at the moment. Her vision had returned to its blurred state. She didn't worry about it too much. It had reappeared with vivid crispness several times during the past couple of days. The clarity stayed longer and came with more frequency each time. She prayed her vision would return in full at some point, but she'd adapted to not seeing, too.

She hadn't spent much time with God lately. The realization caused a catch in her heart. Her prayers at the moment were rote, but she told herself she'd do better in the future. She'd spent most of her time during the past three years just existing. Her uncle had to be very disappointed. He'd told her as much, but in her newly blind state, she hadn't really cared. And ever since, she'd drifted away from everyone except her father. And now he'd somehow drifted away from her. Maybe God was trying to get her attention.

The briny scent of the sea and the taste of salt on her lips reassured her that not everything had changed. But without her father, Hollan's small world would never be the same. Two facts prevailed and tried to drag her down into depression. Her vision had faded, and her father hadn't returned. She fought hard to keep her positive outlook, but it all felt so confusing.

While the familiar scents and sounds reassured, a tremor started at her leg and steadily worked its way through her stiff body. She wasn't cold. The warmth of the early autumn sun beat down on her shoulders. She wrapped her arms tightly around her torso, as if the action could stop the shaking. She was afraid that if she let go, she'd fall into a million pieces.

A bark in the distance announced Samson's arrival. Hollan whistled for him, and he barked a response. A few moments later, he brushed up against her. His panting gave away the exertion of his latest hunt.

"Still no sign of Papa, Sam?"

The dog only whined and leaned against her thigh. If Samson had found his master, he'd have let Hollan know.

"I didn't think so, boy, but we'll be fine. I still feel confident that Papa's out there somewhere." She reached down to rub his head. And they *would* be okay. Just as soon as she figured out a way to take over her father's job as lightkeeper, her life would steady and move forward again.

Hollan had no idea how long she stood there, staring sightlessly at the water, but when dark clouds covered the warmth of the sun, and dampness from the brisk ocean breeze permeated the light cotton of her long dress, the tremors turned to shivers of cold, and she urged Samson to move back toward their home.

My home, she corrected herself, her steps slow and careful. Now that she was alone—and until her father returned— she was in desperate need of a plan. She passed through the shadow of the lighthouse and raised a hand to caress the cool stone of its base. The lighthouse had remained dark through the majority of the war. They'd only recently resumed operations. She'd need to go up there soon and ready things for the night's work. Whenever her vision cleared, she hurried around and did everything necessary for the next few hours.

She'd spent enough time in the lighthouse to do the basic chores even with her limited sight. When her vision dimmed, she was forced to let the lighthouse sit in darkness, too.

But first she needed to prepare a missive for her uncle. She continued toward the cottage, counting backward through the past few days. The supply boat—if it had fared well through the storm—would arrive later that afternoon. When the young captain, Fletcher, found her alone, he'd surely insist on bringing her back to the mainland. She'd argue with him, and he'd agree to search the island for her father, but after, even if she talked him out of forcing her away, she'd only have a day's worth of time to plan before her uncle descended.

The abrupt pain of her bare foot stubbing against the lowest stone step of the cottage pulled her from her musings. She reached forward to catch her balance against the wooden door, barely preventing a headfirst tumble into the garden to her left. The pain was intense, and she clenched her teeth, blowing a few panting breaths through tight lips to ward off the ache before tentatively putting weight on the aching appendage. She'd likely bruised some toes, but they'd soon be fine as long as she was careful. Though her vision was steadily improving, she needed to pay more attention to her surroundings.

A wry smile formed on her lips as she clung to the solidity of the door and hobbled up the final two steps. Hadn't her father said the same thing to her many times before? The thought brought him closer. Perhaps he wasn't so very far away. His words and teachings, especially the ones about Jesus and His unfailing presence lived on inside her. The thought brought her a moment of peace, but the reality of the reason for the thought again caused tears to threaten. She'd never before been alone. Though she was strong and resilient, she needed to have someone close by. Her father had taught her that with Jesus as her Savior, she'd never be truly alone. But while that was all good and well during his suppertime teachings, it didn't really seem to help right now when she lived alone in darkness and needed to find her way.

She shook away the panicked thoughts and chastised herself. More importantly, she needed to write her note before giving in to the cloying and ever-present grief and concern about her missing father.

The wind blew harder, and Hollan hurried to open the door, suddenly anxious to be safely tucked inside the dimly lit interior of the cottage. Samson nudged in front of her and trotted to his usual position near the dying embers of the fireplace. Hollan closed and secured the door then felt her way across the room until she bumped into the small dining table nestled against the far wall. She reached forward and located the lamp with one hand while the fingers of her other hand searched along the rough wood of the table for the nearby matches. The familiar routine soothed her.

Light flared, and she tested her eyes. Though she could see a dim outline of most items in the room, she couldn't see anything clearly.

She moved a few feet across the floor to the hearth and nudged Samson out of the way before leaning down—mindful of her dress hem—to carefully stoke the fire. Years of practice made the chore easy, and she took a few moments to bask in the warmth of the crackling wood. When the flames had dried her dress and heated her skin, she sighed and moved to sit at her small writing table, ready to carefully formulate the brief note for her uncle. The change from the light of the fire to the dimmer light of her writing table didn't help her mission. But in all reality, it didn't matter. Even without the contrast of moving from the bright fire to the blank paper, she could just barely see well enough to discern the letters as she formed them on the blank page. Though not an easy task, she did her best to make the note brief and her correspondence legible.

She considered walking down to the dock to meet Fletcher but decided it was best to wait for him to come to her while she rested her throbbing toes. If she were to stumble or get hurt on the path, it would only fuel Fletcher's potential determination to take her back with him. Instead, she'd sit tight and pray, with the hope that God would answer her prayer by providing her with a way to remain on the island.

two

Jacob topped a slight rise and reined in his horse, scowling as he took in the view spread before him. He'd come home. He ignored the anxiety that invaded his thoughts as he contemplated the hostile reception he might receive and instead focused on the beauty of his surroundings. He'd missed the ocean. And if he had to admit it to himself, deep down he was glad to be back.

He had a lot of wrongs to right, and after one quick stop, he'd start the process with Hollan.

The dirt path he'd traveled led directly to the thin strip of water that separated the mainland from Little Cumberland Island. A larger dirt road bisected the path, leading to the tiny village where he'd grown up. Small fishing vessels bobbed on the dark blue water, each one filled with occupants in various stages of securing their catch. The fishermen pulled nets laden with their bounty from the salty water, while others prepared to toss their nets back in from a better vantage point. A few scattered figures walked along the shore, enjoying the brilliant day, some feeding the seagulls and others looking for seashells. Out on the island, the lighthouse stood tall on the distant horizon, keeping watch over the mouth of the Satilla River and the coast.

Jacob figured he should feel some sort of reluctance at the thought of returning home to the seaside town as a prodigal of sorts, but instead relief loosened the tightness from his shoulders now that he'd arrived at his destination. His burden felt much lighter.

Three years earlier, he'd left his hometown behind. By day he'd lived life as a traveling preacher. At night he'd scoured the surrounding towns, looking for his outlaw father and brothers. In both endeavors, he'd been full of expectations and enthusiasm. Yet life on the road had left him surprisingly empty and alone. He'd thought doing the Lord's work would bring him contentment no matter where he was and that by bringing his family to justice he would in some way undo the evils they'd committed. But instead the process had drained him.

He had one more brother to track, but for longer than he wanted to admit, the tug to return home had consumed him. When his brother's trail turned and led toward home, Jacob felt the first flicker of hope in a long time. He knew God had a plan for his return. And now that Jacob had returned, for the first time in a long time he felt reassuring peace flow through him. He felt confident that he'd soon locate David and that justice would prevail.

Jacob turned the horse and urged him toward the village. First order of business was to find his good friend and advisor, Edward Poe. He'd start at the tiny parsonage. Jacob held his head high as he rode, not missing the glances that followed his progress as he passed, nor did he miss the way the townspeople bent their heads close together to whisper as he moved by.

The double doors at the front of the small whitewashed church were propped wide open, and they welcomed Jacob inside. He swung down from his horse with a smile, secured him to one of the hitching posts that stood sentry under the shady magnolias flanking both sides of the front steps, and pulled his hat from his head. As he walked he slapped the dusty brim against his equally dusty pants in a vain effort to shake off the remnants of the trail. With a sense of anticipation, he moved forward and entered the cool interior of the worn clapboard building.

Edward sat at a small table in an alcove just inside the front of the church. He had one elbow propped against the surface, his hand resting against his forehead while his other hand clutched an open note. The parson's eyes were closed and his white-topped head bowed in apparent prayer over the missive.

Jacob remained silent until Edward lifted his head, finally aware of his presence.

"Jacob Swan!" Hurrying to his feet, Edward came forward and pulled Jacob into a warm embrace. "You've come home. After all this time and those few notes insinuating your intent, you finally followed through!"

"I did indeed." Jacob smiled at his mentor. "I couldn't find peace on the trail and decided I'd best come back before the good Lord found a more blunt way to send me home to my roots."

Jacob stood with arms crossed and feet squared and grinned at his favorite teacher.

Edward studied him. "You had some concerns about your return. Have those worries lessened?"

Jacob shook his head. He tried to fight off the urge to pace but finally gave in and moved a few steps away and back in the small space behind the pews. Edward followed his movements with knowing eyes.

"You're nervous about your reception."

Jacob glanced out the church doors, watching as a couple of people moved past the entrance. "I am. It's the only thing that's held me back from coming sooner. My family. . ."

"Your family made their choices, Jacob. Those choices weren't yours, and the people around here all know it."

"I'm not sure my neighbors will see it that way. The

townspeople are already talking."

"Well, that's their problem to live with until they see the truth. And you know how they love to talk. In the meantime, all that matters is that you've come home. I know several people who will rejoice at that news, Ettie being one of them."

Jacob smiled at Edward's mention of his wife. "I look forward to seeing her. Before I do any visiting, though, I need to finish some details of my return. I'll need a place to live. I need to locate work—and even though you think my father's and brothers' actions won't be held against me, I suspect I'll have a hard time securing a job."

"Tell me something." Edward frowned as he mulled over Jacob's words. "With all your concerns, why did you come back?"

"The Lord called me here. I stayed away until I couldn't refuse, if that makes any sense. The past year has been hard. Each time I tried to ignore the quiet voice urging me to return, things became harder on the circuit. I'm tired, and I need a change. More than anything, I want to right my brothers' wrongs. I want to make up for my father's poor choices."

"I see." Edward nodded. "That's a pretty strong order. But to put things in perspective, it's not uncommon for a traveling preacher to wear out if he doesn't take time to stoke the fire—especially if he's chasing his own demons at the same time." He sent Jacob another knowing look. "And after so many years on the road, giving to everyone you come across, you need to be refreshed. You need a break, yet you need to find a way into the hearts and lives of the locals." He glanced at the note on the table, and his features transformed with excitement. "And I think I have just the solution."

Jacob's eyes narrowed. Edward's *solutions* always came with a price. Sometimes a very high price.

"Don't look so suspicious." Edward clapped him on the back and motioned to the rear pew. "I think your timely arrival might just be an answer to my prayer. Sit."

Jacob sat. How he'd gone from confident warrior to submissive schoolboy in a few short moments he didn't know.

Edward joined him. "You're not sure what the towns-people's feelings will be now that you've returned. Correct?"

"Yeeesss." Jacob drawled the word out, knowing his agreement came with a catch.

"If you were to marry one of the town's darlings, it would go a long way in clearing the path toward your redemption, would it not?"

"Marriage?" Jacob's voice rose in volume and pitch. He jumped to his feet, ready to flee. "You just said my family's actions were not my own. Now you're using the situation against me to force me into marriage?"

"You know I wouldn't force you to do anything."

"I didn't come home to marry."

"I'm sorry. Is there someone else, another woman who holds your heart?" Edward asked in surprise. "Is this the cause of your return?"

"Another woman? Of course not! You know there is only one woman for me. The only woman I'll ever love is Hollan. And my father's and brothers' actions ended any chance for that marriage. After what they did to Hollan and her family. . ." He shook his head. "I can't believe you asked if there was anyone else. I'm constantly on the move. When would I have time to build a relationship with a woman? There's no one out there waiting for me. My family's legacy chases away any desire I might have to marry." He ignored Edward's motion that he be seated and paced the room again. "Marriage is the furthest thing from my mind."

"You have no intention of settling down?"

"I do want to settle down. I just prefer to settle alone."

"And there's no one—besides Hollan—who holds your heart?"

Jacob hesitated before answering. He had a feeling his words were throwing him headfirst into Edward's plans. "No. You know my father was an evil man. I watched my father's actions pull the life from my mother. I watched him break my brothers with his cruelty and then watched my brothers hurt the women in their paths. I won't do that to anyone else."

"How many times do I have to remind you? You aren't your father or your brothers."

"I understand that, but I am my father's son. My brothers treated the women in their lives in the same exact manner as my father treated my mother. Or should I say, *mistreated*."

"You didn't agree with your family's lack of morals back then. Why do you think you'd be like them now?"

"I won't marry, Edward. I won't take on a carefree bride, just to make her into a miserable wife."

Edward's face fell. "I see."

Jacob stopped in his tracks, suspicious at his mentor's abrupt change of heart. It wasn't like him to give up so easily. Whatever Edward needed must be very important to him. And Jacob owed the man. . .owed him a lot. When all the other people in town turned their backs on him, Edward had given Jacob a home. More importantly, from the time he was a boy, Edward had taught Jacob about his faith. He'd shaped Jacob's whole future from that of an outlaw to one as God's chosen. He and Ettie had encouraged him during the years he fought in the war. There wasn't much Jacob could deny the older man. But marriage?

Jacob battled his inner thoughts and lost.

"What—or who—do you have in mind?" He folded his

arms and spat the words out, hardly the picture of amiability, but marriage was a big request.

Edward walked over to the table and picked up the note. "I received this shortly before you arrived. I've been praying ever since."

Jacob pulled the paper from his mentor's hand and read the words carefully. His heart tightened with each word of the missive. "Hollan."

"Yes, Jacob. And she's all alone. Well, not exactly alone at the moment. I've sent Sylvia over to stay until I could find a better solution."

"Sylvia?"

"Hollan's mother's best friend. She's a widow. The night of your family's rampage, Hollan's mother passed away. Hollan was injured. Sylvia went over to care for Hollan and her father until Hollan could manage alone."

"I remember Sylvia." Jacob winced. "I'm glad she was there for Hollan. I never wanted her hurt."

Edward paused. "You still love Hollan."

"I will always love her, but that night when my family left town, things between us changed." He held out the note for Edward. Edward ignored it, letting the note burn a path through Jacob's fingers. *Hollan had touched this paper.* "Ettie would want to bring her home to the parsonage, wouldn't she?"

Edward nodded. "Of course. And Ettie would be ecstatic at the chance to fuss over Hollan. But do you really think Hollan would be happy with that arrangement? You know my niece. She loves her life on the island. Bringing her here would be the worst thing we could do."

Jacob felt the weight of responsibility press down on him.

"Surely there's another solution. If Sylvia is with her, I could go over and stay at the lighthouse. I could do the necessary work—I often helped Gunter with the lighthouse—while

Hollan could remain in her home." His thoughts made so much sense that the burden lifted. Edward would have to see the perfection in his plan.

"Sylvia can't stay. She's only there for a few days. After that she'll return to the mainland. If I can't find another solution, Hollan will have to return with her. That'll break her heart. And she's already been through so much."

Guilt ricocheted through Jacob's heart. She'd been through so much because of him. If Jacob kept his gaze toward the door, he'd be able to walk away from the situation. His conscience and sense of obligation would likely send him right back in, but he'd have had a chance. Instead he looked into Edward's eyes, and the pleading there settled his fate. He couldn't tell him no. Not after everything Edward had done for him.

"I can't just go out there and man the lighthouse and watch over her from afar?"

"You know people would talk. It would add fuel to the fire regarding your relationship and would tarnish Hollan's reputation. Make things right, Jacob. Go out there and finish what you started."

"Marriage, huh?"

Edward nodded. "It would be the only way, for propriety's sake. And if you truly have no desire to marry for love, a marriage of convenience wouldn't be such a bad thing, would it?"

Jacob shrugged. "The only way I'd ever marry would be for love, but Hollan will never have me. You know how things ended. What my brother did—"

Edward cut him off. "Think about the good that will come of this. With or without this marriage, I'm sure in time you'll find your neighbors' acceptance. Without being married at that time, with your charm and handsome demeanor, the womenfolk will line the eligible ladies up at your door, trying to get you settled. If you marry Hollan, the process of acceptance will move more quickly, without all the matchmaking that will surely come your way."

Jacob shuddered.

Edward took the action as encouragement to continue. "You'll soon be able to relax on the island. You know Hollan is independent and undemanding. The situation will be perfect for both of you."

"Speaking of Hollan, how do you expect her to react when you arrive on the island with her new husband?"

Edward grinned. "She'll be so happy to be able to stay on her beloved island, she'll welcome the idea with open arms. She once loved you, Jacob. She'll soon learn to love you again. I'll explain things to her as soon as we arrive. She'll embrace the idea."

Jacob raised his hands in surrender. "I guess you'd best prepare to board my horse."

three

"We're doing *what?*" Hollan's words ended in a shriek. "I—you—what? No. No! I won't do this. You want me to marry a complete *stranger?*"

"Jacob's hardly a stranger, Hollan. You two were engaged. You've known him since you were young."

"Oh yes. I remember. Right before he ran off with his outlaw family after they pillaged the town. The night my mother. . ." Hollan let her voice drift away as she stomped away from her uncle and headed for her place of refuge— the sand dune overlooking the ocean—wanting to leave everyone behind. Her astute hearing told her that her uncle ignored the fact that she'd purposely left him in her dust and continued to follow along.

"He didn't run off with them. He went after them to bring them to justice."

Hollan spun to face him. "How can you want this for me? How will this *fix* my present situation? Our love disappeared along with him the night he left. An arrangement like this will only bring more problems." She figured her horrified words could be heard all the way to the mainland, but she didn't care. What was her uncle thinking? "There must be another way."

Her uncle raised his gentle voice so he could be heard above the wind that blew in off the water. "I'm open to suggestions, Hollan. You need to be reasonable. You know you can't stay out here alone. Do you have a better plan?"

Hollan would find one. She had to. Anything was better

than an arranged marriage to someone she no longer knew. The man she'd known no longer existed, if he ever had. She hadn't seen Jacob in years. The night he left, Hollan had lost her mother, her vision, and Jacob's love. It was a night she never wanted to think about again.

The man had outlaw roots, plain and simple, and in the end, when it mattered the most, those outlaw tendencies seemed to come to the forefront. Why else would he run off with his outlaw family and leave her to pick up the pieces? It didn't matter how long or how well Uncle Edward had known the man. Hollan didn't want any part of this.

Soon after Jacob had left—after she'd recovered from her accident—she'd made the decision to never marry. With her visual difficulties, she'd feel like a burden in the eyes of whoever ended up with her. She'd lose her independence. Her mother had unraveled on that horrible night, and she could only imagine why. If her mother had been happy, why would she have jumped from the lighthouse?

For her uncle to be desperate enough to marry her off to an outlaw, she was in a worse situation than she'd ever imagined. Marriage in any situation wasn't a good idea, but this was oh-so-much worse.

"How can you not see that this isn't an option for me?" Her mother's desperate attempt to escape from their life closed the door on that idea for Hollan years ago.

"Your mother wasn't of sound mind, Hollan. The accident wasn't what you think. Your parents had a wonderful marriage."

"What changed that? If something could go so horribly wrong in their marriage, how am I to know the same thing won't happen to me?" A balmy wind blew around her. She breathed in the comforting scent. "And I already come along with enough of my own challenges—challenges that would cause undue burden even in the strongest of marriages. Even in a marriage filled with love, which this one won't have."

"The two of you loved each other before. I know you can find your way back to each other and love again. As for your mother's accident, we do need to discuss it further, but now isn't the time. Just know her decision that night had nothing to do with her love for you or your father." Her uncle's speech ended, and he stood silently beside her.

Her father and Sylvia both wrote Hollan's mother's demise off to an unstable mind, but she couldn't understand that. Why hadn't her father been able to fix whatever was wrong? Why hadn't the need to be around for Hollan been enough to keep her mother's mind intact? What could be so awful that her mother thought the answer lay in plummeting from the deck that ran around the lighthouse? In any case, her family history didn't bode well for marriage, especially when marriage to her came with the additional challenge of dealing with a sightless wife.

Well, she amended, her heart jumping with a momentary lilt—*a partially sightless wife.* Her vision still improved daily, returning in bits and pieces. Even now she could see the outline of Sylvia's slightly curved figure to her left and her uncle's more barrel-shaped chest to her right. A bit of a distance away, the bright midmorning sun highlighted the tall figure of her husband-to-be.

Hollan turned toward her caretaker. "Sylvia, you'll stay on to help me, won't you? I'll make sure you're well paid for your time. And Fletcher can take over the lighthouse. You know you're both welcome here."

Fletcher was a good man and a hard worker. After dropping off her uncle and Jacob, he left with the supply boat to fulfill his normal workday, even after the long night of tending to the lighthouse.

Sylvia moved forward to place a reassuring hand against

Hollan's cheek. "You know I can't stay, dear. We've had this talk. I'm needed in town, and Fletcher's work doesn't allow him to be out here on the island. He can't continue to work the lighthouse *and* run the boat. You'll be fine with your uncle's arrangement. You know he wouldn't do anything to hurt you."

"But Sylvia, I—"

Her caretaker dropped her voice to a whisper and leaned close as if Hollan hadn't spoken. "And we all know how much that man over there once loved you. You'll find your way back to him again." She planted a soft kiss on Hollan's cheek and moved back toward the house.

"But—Sylvia! Wait."

"I can't, darling. I need to pack up and be ready to go when Fletcher returns."

"Argh!" Hollan stomped her foot.

The action was rewarded with a deep chuckle from up the hill. *Jacob. The heartbreaking outlaw.* She ignored him and spun back around to her uncle.

"An outlaw, Uncle Edward? Is that really what my future has come to? Am I such a burden that only he will take me?"

"I don't consider you to be a burden at all. As a matter of fact, your aunt Ettie and I would like nothing more than to have you pack up and return to the mainland to stay with us. We can forget this conversation ever happened, and you can start anew in our home. You do have a choice."

Hollan turned away so he'd not see her face crumple at the dismal choices set before her. She loved her uncle and aunt, but she loved her island, too. "Marriage to an outlaw or I leave the only home I've ever known to start over again in town. And what a choice it is."

"Don't sound so despondent, dear one. You know I'd never do anything to hurt you. And Jacob isn't an outlaw."

"The history of the Swan family made it all the way out here, Uncle. I know what his family did."

"Their history isn't Jacob's. You knew him as a boy and as a young man. He's a good person. That hasn't changed. He wasn't with his brothers or father when they pillaged and set fire that night. Their actions have caused him enough pain, and I won't have you joining in with the townsfolk and judging him unfairly. Jacob is a wonderful man of God. He wants nothing more than to live in peace, free from the demons that pursue him. He only seeks quiet and relaxation. The marriage will be in name only, for propriety's sake. You both seem determined in your quest to avoid marriage. Perhaps this arrangement will protect you from the very institution you both abhor."

Hollan couldn't help but laugh. "Marriage will protect us from marriage? That makes no sense."

"Nothing much makes sense lately, Hollan." Her uncle sighed. "But if you're both sure you don't want to seek out love and settle down with someone else—someone else you care deeply for—then this arrangement is for the best. You'll have the protection you require and, in exchange, someone to run the lighthouse."

"And what will Jacob get?"

"The quiet life on the island will agree with Jacob and will salve the scars of his past. I have no doubt he'll like it here. The two of you loved each other before. I know you'll take care of each other, even if your love is gone. You'll see the good in him. And in time the townspeople will see it, too."

Hollan started to ask what scars he carried but figured with his family history it was obvious. When Jacob went to serve in the war, his brothers and father had evaded any type of service. They'd been suspected of pillaging and raiding local towns instead.

"If you don't want to agree to this arrangement, you'll need to head up to the house and pack your things. We'll leave late afternoon when Fletcher returns for his mother."

"I marry Jacob, or I leave the island." The whispered words blew away on the breeze. "I can't leave my island. It's all Samson and I have left. It's our home."

"Then you agree to the marriage?"

She thought hard, but no better solution came to her. "Yes, Uncle Edward. Prepare the way for my wedding. I guess I'll marry the outlaw."

"You'll marry a gentleman. I'll have you see it no other way."

"Perhaps you should reintroduce me to my groom." She folded her arms at her chest and refused to turn around to see if Jacob stood nearby. "Is he still standing on the hill listening?"

Her uncle chuckled. "No, he fled after your foot stomp. He's down the beach a bit with Samson."

"With Samson? The traitor."

They fell into step together and headed in that direction. The sound of the surf rose in volume as they neared the shore. Hollan's bare feet sank into the soft sand, and an impetuous thought made her smile. What would her new husband think of her perpetually shoeless state? Perhaps he'd never know. But with the loss of her sight, she needed to use each and every sense she could. She loved to feel the textures of the ground around her. And she found the sensation of sand beneath her toes to be her favorite sensation of all. She wouldn't have that pleasure in town. She'd made the right decision, even if it was scary and hard.

She stopped momentarily to breathe in the always-present, reassuring scent of her surroundings. Marriage couldn't be worse than losing the island. She'd come through this and be just fine on the other side. She was not her mother.

Her uncle's voice broke into her musings. "Samson seems content. He's retrieving sticks thrown into the water by Jacob. Maybe the animal sees the merit of the situation better than you do."

"Samson doesn't make up with anyone, Uncle Edward. You know that. All the changes of late must be muddling his little doggy brain."

"That dog has more brain than most men I know, your fiancé not included."

"My fiancé." She groaned.

"Your fiancé only for a short while." Her uncle's voice held a hint of laughter. "Before you have a chance to get used to the idea, your fiancé will be your spouse."

"Maybe I could have a bit more time to get used to the fiancé angle before we jump into marriage?" she asked hopefully.

"Take all the time you need. After reintroductions, you'll have the better part of the next hour to get used to the spouse part of the idea. You'll get through this just fine."

Hollan stopped, and Samson ran to her side. She ran a clammy hand self-consciously through her wind-tossed hair. The hot sun beat down on her back. What must her husband-to-be think of her? Did he, too, see the ceremony as "something to get through"? Would he someday mourn his loss of choice in handpicking a bride in the future? He'd already turned his back on her once. Would he spend the rest of his life regretting her?

She squared her shoulders and moved forward. She wouldn't be pathetic. Her fiancé would meet the independent woman who was his future wife.

four

"Jacob, Hollan thought it best that you meet again before you marry."

The introduction felt odd, but as Edward led the beautiful but reluctant woman closer, Jacob realized she might as well be a stranger to him. Hollan had matured and grown even more beautiful, something he hadn't thought possible three short years earlier. She wore her auburn hair pulled up, but stray wisps blew around her face. She reached up to hold them tentatively away from her delicate features. He saw only a glimpse of her warm brown eyes before she looked away.

Jacob wondered if she felt as awkward in the situation as he did. Outwardly she seemed completely calm, but judging by her earlier response, she, too, felt the tension. And how could she not? Her life had taken on a myriad of changes in a very short time.

"Hollan." Jacob stepped forward. "The years have been good to you. I'm pleased to see you again." He winced. Perhaps those weren't the best choice of words to say to someone who'd lost most everything they valued.

She reached a dainty hand his way, and he took it briefly in his own. She looked toward him, though her eyes didn't meet his. A slight smile tilted up the corners of her mouth as her chin dipped in a nod of acknowledgment. "I'm pleased to meet you again, too." The forced smile stayed in place as she bit out each word.

Jacob held back the laugh that threatened at her forced words. He wouldn't do anything to jeopardize their future together, but she was anything *but* pleased. Her choices had been reduced to a life in town away from everything she knew and loved or a life married to—as far as she was concerned—a complete and total stranger who had already wreaked havoc in her life once before. That their marriage came with her uncle's blessing didn't really matter at this point—he was a stranger to her all the same.

An unexpectedly protective urge slammed through him as he held her soft hand in his, even as he felt the strength in her own response. She squeezed his hand once and released him.

"I'll leave you two to get acquainted. I have several things to attend to before we do the ceremony."

Jacob didn't miss the momentary panic that moved across Hollan's face. She wasn't as calm as she tried to let on. He'd do his best to put her at ease, but in reality he was just as nervous and shaken up.

They stood quietly for a few moments as her uncle made his retreat. Jacob loved the man, owed him his life, and would do everything in his power to make things easier for his former fiancée.

"Shall we walk?"

"Walk?" Hollan stuttered over the word, glancing up the coast.

"You know, one foot in front of the other as we move along the shore?" He figured the distraction of movement would be better than awkwardly standing there. "We should at least try to get acquainted as your uncle suggested. It's been a long time. We have a lot to discuss."

"I suppose."

"If I may?" He reached for her hand and placed it against his bent arm. She stiffened, and he thought she might pull away, but then she relaxed and accepted his assistance. He felt the heat from her fingers through the rolled-up sleeves of his thin cotton shirt. The sensation was pleasantly familiar. He'd missed her touch. He suddenly realized this wouldn't be nearly as easy as he'd imagined. The heart of stone he'd envisioned at his core was suddenly turning to mush.

They began to walk, and he took care not to let the waves break against her long dark skirt. A few times he led her higher up the beach to avoid an especially aggressive wave.

"What did you want to talk about?"

"Guidelines." Which, based on his response to her touch, they now needed worse than ever.

Her brows drew together. Her hand tightened against his arm, and her steps faltered. "Guidelines? Such as?"

"I know you aren't exactly excited about this arrangement."

He hesitated when she laughed.

"That's an understatement." Remorse immediately replaced the smile. "I'm sorry. It can't be much easier for you. You're making a great sacrifice and doing me a huge favor by allowing me to remain here, for reasons I can't even imagine."

The way his emotions were tossing about—much like the faraway ship moved across the storm-tossed sea—it didn't make marriage to her feel like such a sacrifice. He cleared his throat. "I'll be fine. But I want you to have peace with the situation, at least as much peace as possible. I want to do what I can to make the adjustment easier for us both."

She stopped. "Why are you doing this? What's in it for you? I want to hear your reasons from you."

"I think that answer is obvious. I know your uncle went over it with you. But to reiterate, we each have something the other needs."

"And what would that be?"

He reached for her wrist as she pulled away. Her rapid pulse beat against his fingers. He prayed for the words that would help soothe her fears as he again tucked her hand firmly in place. They continued walking at a leisurely pace.

"You aren't the only one who's had a rough time of it. You know I owe your uncle a great deal. I owe you, too. The night I left town, after what my family did, I couldn't face you. I needed to get away." He didn't really want to hear the specific details of what his brothers had done, but he left her the opportunity to discuss that night if she needed to. Otherwise, the details would come out in time.

"And yet you've returned."

"Yes." He was surprised she didn't lash out or want to discuss the details. But perhaps she'd never want to discuss it. He glanced down at the sand as they walked, and a delicate shell caught his attention. He bent to pick it up. Most of the shells on the beach had been broken into jagged pieces by the strong tides before they ever finished their tumble to shore. He started to throw his find into the ocean, but instead he carried it as they walked along, turning the smooth object over and over with his fingers. This shell, which looked so delicate, had to be strong to have made it through the rough waters in one piece. It reminded him of the woman who walked beside him. "The trails didn't hold the answers I'd hoped for."

"And you expect to find the answers out here?"

"The answers will come in time. Here I'll find quiet and relaxation. At least that's what Edward tells me." He grinned her way, even though she wouldn't notice. The smile carried on his words. "I suppose that remains to be seen."

Judging by the effect the gently breaking waves about a dozen feet out were having on him, Uncle Edward was correct. He felt a peace here he hadn't felt on the mainland. Or maybe it was the gentle nature of the woman walking beside him that charmed his heart. He hoped the feeling was mutual.

"I won't get in your way."

Not quite the response he'd envisioned and hoped for.

"I don't want you to avoid me. I don't want to force any changes on you."

"What *do* you want from me?"

"Pardon?"

"What are your expectations?"

"I have no expectations. I haven't had time to think of any."

"I guess that's true. Where do you plan to sleep?"

Again she had him grinning. "You don't tiptoe around your thoughts, do you?" He hadn't smiled this much in years.

"I try not to. You know my father. He taught me that if a question is good enough to think about, it's worthy of putting into words."

His father's teachings had been far different. "I always liked your father. But to answer your question"—he turned back and glanced at the lighthouse—"your uncle said there's a room at the base of the lighthouse that would serve well as my living quarters."

Her features relaxed as she released a soft sigh. He hadn't noticed she'd been holding her breath while waiting for his answer.

"Indeed. He's right. That will work out nicely. The room is already set up with a bed. My father would often stay out there during difficult weather. Except for the night he disappeared." Her voice tapered off. A scowl marred her features.

"Fletcher said he searched the island."

"He did. But I don't feel as if my father is gone." Her grip tightened against his arm. "When my mother—died, after I came to, I knew instantly that she was no longer with us."

"I'll continue to look for him. If he's here, we'll find him."

"Thank you." For the first time her smile appeared to

be genuine. "Fletcher and Sylvia seem to think it's shock talking when I say that. My uncle surely thinks the same." She shrugged.

They turned and headed back toward the cottage, the silence around them broken only by the cries of the seagulls.

She abruptly appeared to shake off the melancholy mood along with whatever thoughts were on her mind by quickly changing the subject. "I'll make your meals of course."

"That would be nice."

A most charming blush colored her cheeks. "You can eat in your room or up in the lighthouse if you'd prefer, but I won't mind if you'd like to join me at mealtime, either. I'd appreciate the company." She dropped her hand from his arm and hugged her arms around her torso.

Though in all likelihood she was only trying to be charitable in order to please her uncle, and judging from her actions hoped he'd say no, he couldn't stop the words that instantly popped out in response to her invitation. "I'd like that."

"You would?" Surprised, she stumbled and would have fallen had he not grabbed her by the arm. "Well, then. . . ouch!"

He'd been so mesmerized by Hollan and her enticing personality that he hadn't paid enough attention to all the broken shells and the uneven shoreline on this part of the beach. He should have been more diligent. Edward was counting on him to keep Hollan safe.

"What happened?"

"I'm fine." She waved him away, a look of desperation on her face as she tilted her head and listened to the sounds.

Jacob could only hear the surf breaking at their feet along with the calls of seagulls from up ahead.

"We're almost back to the cottage. Sylvia has been feeding

the gulls about this time every day, and I can hear them begging up near the lighthouse." She took a cautious step, gasped, and closed her eyes in pain.

"You're hurt. Let me have a look."

"No."

"You're soon to be my wife. I don't think it will hurt for me to take a look. One of the shells must have cut through your boot."

"I'm not wearing any boots." She sighed. Frustrated, she scrunched her fingers in her hair. More loosened tendrils of auburn hair blew around her face. "I like to feel the sand under my feet."

She started when he laughed out loud.

"You find the notion funny?"

"I find you to be quite funny." He scooped her up in his arms and carried her away from the shells.

"I beg your pardon! Jacob, put me down!"

He had no intention of putting her down. She felt too good in his arms. "I will as soon as we get past these broken shells." He settled her on a large piece of driftwood before dropping to his knees in the sand. "Let me see the damage."

With a sigh she allowed him to look at her foot.

"There's still a fragment embedded in your skin. You're bleeding. No wonder it hurt to walk." He gently tugged the shell loose, but Hollan still gasped and patted at his arm.

"Ah, that hurt!"

"Sorry. The fragment is out now, but you can't walk on your foot. You'll fill the cut with sand. Stay put for a moment." He pulled a handkerchief from his pocket and walked down to dip it in the water.

Hollan stood, apparently planning to follow him.

Some things never changed.

"Must you always be so stubborn?" he called. She'd been an

opinionated handful since the first day he'd met her. "I said to stay put. The last thing you need is an infection, and these shells can give you a pretty nasty one if you aren't careful."

He hurried to where she'd settled back down on the log.

"And you're as boorish as ever." She crossed her arms as she huffed out the words.

He brushed at the wound, but the sand wouldn't come free. "I'm going to have to carry you back down to the water. You'll need to hold your skirt up while I dip your foot in the ocean."

"You'll do no such thing. If you'll lend me your handkerchief, I can make a bandage. When we get back to the cottage, I'll make a poultice out of herbs."

"I'm sure you will, and that'll be fine, just as soon as we get all the sand out." He didn't give her a chance to argue as he lifted her up in his arms.

"Put me down," she hissed.

He walked to the water's edge. "Ready?"

"No."

Ignoring her, he dipped her foot into the ocean, soaking her skirt hem with seawater in the process. "There. That ought to do it."

"My skirt is drenched."

"I said you'd need to hold it up."

She glared his way. "And I *said* I wasn't ready."

"Would you have ever been ready?"

"No."

"Exactly."

She balanced on one foot until an overzealous wave knocked her backward. Jacob steadied her.

Her breath came in small huffy bursts. She was angry.

"Now see?" She poked him in the chest with her index finger. "This is exactly the behavior I worried would come along with our marriage."

"If you're referring to the fact that I just cleaned your wound and saved you from a tumble in the water, your worries are for naught. Speaking of our marriage, you might have all the time in the world to stand here and argue, but I have a wedding to attend."

"Unfortunately, so do I, and I'm going to arrive looking like a drowned rat."

"I recall asking if you were ready."

"And I *recall* saying no." She started to hobble up the shore.

"Stubborn woman! You're going to get the wound full of sand again."

"I'll—"

He didn't give her a chance to finish. Instead he flung her over his shoulder like a sack of potatoes. She shrieked and pummeled him on the back as he stalked up the path with long strides.

He might as well face her uncle head-on. At the rate they were going, the wedding was likely off anyway. Jacob didn't like the thought. He still had feelings for the feisty woman in his arms. But less than an hour earlier, Edward had entrusted into Jacob's care a healthy, pristine niece. Jacob now returned her injured, wet, and angry. The whole ordeal was anything but peaceful and relaxing. In all honesty, dealing with the townspeople couldn't possibly be any more frustrating than this.

Jacob didn't relish the thought of facing her uncle with his obvious failure, but the sooner they got the ordeal over with, the sooner they could put this mistake behind them.

five

Uncle Edward's booming laugh welcomed them back to the cottage. Hollan didn't need to see his face—a feat that would be impossible even if she could see, thanks to her present dangling-upside-down-over-Jacob's-shoulder position—to know that the laughter was at her expense.

"I'm thrilled that you find my situation so immensely amusing, but perhaps you could stop laughing long enough to make him put me down." Her indignation was wasted on the man. She couldn't be heard over the laughter with her face and voice muffled against the back of Jacob's shirt. She tried to ignore the strength of his muscles, but it was hard to do while feeling the solid resistance as she again pummeled her fists against his back.

Jacob apparently heard. Or maybe the hard pinch to his side alerted him to her fury. He dumped her unceremoniously on her feet, only mindful at the last moment of her injury. "Thought I was going to drop you on your sore foot, didn't you?"

His voice was low, for her ears only, and she shivered at the intimacy. His closeness unnerved her. She limped a few steps away.

"You're hurt!" Immediately contrite, her uncle appeared at her side.

"Of course I'm hurt. Do you think I'd let him carry me up the dunes in that humiliating manner for the fun of it?" She sent another ferocious glare in Jacob's general direction. She didn't miss his chuckle.

"She hardly *let* me do anything. I had to take matters

38

into my own hands. And it's only a surface wound, Edward, nothing to be alarmed about. Hollan will be fine."

"*Only* a surface wound? At the beach you acted as if I'd bleed to death without your immediate intervention."

"No, I only said the wound would fill with sand and increase the risk of infection, which reminds me, you do need to let Sylvia apply that herbal poultice."

"Help her over to this chair, Jacob, and we'll get her taken care of." Edward summoned Sylvia, and after a quick peek at the wound, she hurried off for the supplies. "Fletcher arrived at the dock just before you two made your appearance. He should be here shortly. As soon as he is, we'll get this wedding started."

Hollan sputtered. "You mean you're still planning the wedding, even after all this?"

"Indeed. Why wouldn't I? Jacob just proved he could deal with you quite nicely."

"Deal with me? You consider slinging me over his shoulder against my wishes *dealing with me nicely*?"

"Compared to the alternative, yes. The gash isn't life threatening, but walking on it wouldn't have been wise at all. Jacob made the best decision for you, based on the options."

Hollan snorted and shifted in her chair, turning her back on both of them.

"Dear, have you changed your mind?" She heard concern buried beneath the humor as her uncle placed a hand on her shoulder. "If so, you can pack a small bag and leave on the boat with us. We can collect the rest of your things later. Jacob can stay and tend to the light."

Hollan considered his offer. The emotions she felt when Jacob stood nearby concerned her more than any of his actions. She knew he had only her best interests at heart. But she hadn't expected the old feelings to come rushing back in such a vivid way. A part of her she'd thought long dead had come back alive in his presence. The realization scared and unnerved her.

"No, I'll be fine." And she would be. She wasn't leaving her island. Samson plopped down beside her with a contented sigh, breaking the awkward moment. "Samson seems happy enough to hear he still has a home."

"He could have stayed out here with me." Jacob stood nearby, listening.

Hollan wished she could see Jacob's expression. Was he disappointed she hadn't taken her uncle up on his offer? Would he have preferred to stay at the lighthouse alone? She thought about it a moment and decided she didn't care. She hadn't made him come out to get hitched, and if he had his doubts, they were his problem to deal with.

"Aunt Ettie's going to be upset about missing the ceremony." She addressed the statement to her uncle.

"I asked if she wanted to come, but she was so sure you'd turn us down flat, I couldn't get her in the boat."

"She still hates it out here. She's never cared for the island."

"She loved your mother like a sister. And though she wanted to be here with you, she can't deal with coming to the island just yet. I think she fully expected you to return to the house with me."

"I understand. Tell her I'll be in to see her soon."

"She'll want to have you both over for dinner."

"We'd like that." Jacob spoke for them both. "Ettie is a wonderful cook."

Hollan wondered about the fact that it didn't bother her that he spoke of them as a couple. Instead, it felt natural. Comforting.

Sylvia arrived and busied herself with tending to the cut. Fletcher arrived at the cottage, and the men exited and walked over to the dunes. A short time later Sylvia had Hollan bandaged up and ready for the ceremony. She helped Hollan into her prettiest blue dress—a color Hollan belatedly remembered was Jacob's favorite. She blushed, wondering if he'd think she'd chosen it especially for him..

"You look beautiful, Hollan. Your mother would be proud."

Hollan hugged the older woman, not sure she agreed. Her mother would have wanted Hollan to marry for love. They'd talked about it many times before, back in the carefree days when she was happily engaged to Jacob. Though the man remained the same, the circumstances had changed.

When Hollan didn't answer, Sylvia cupped her cheeks. "Your mother would understand."

Hollan nodded her agreement. "I'd like to think so."

"Jacob is a good man. If you give him a chance, he'll make you very happy. I think God has something beautiful planned in all of this."

Though Hollan wasn't so sure about that, she hoped her friend was right.

They decided to say their vows on a dune overlooking the ocean. The whole situation felt surreal. The wedding, although very similar to the one in her dreams—the wedding she'd wanted the first time before Jacob left—seemed a farce. The man standing beside her was nothing more than a stranger, and only a handful of loved ones stood alongside to witness the event.

Other than those few *minor* details, she thought wryly, the afternoon couldn't have been more perfect for their ceremony. Hollan loved being serenaded by the seagulls that flew over their heads. The ever-present sound of the waves crashing onshore brought a familiar comforting reassurance. She knew the sounds inland would be similar—the small village was a coastal town after all—but she wouldn't hear the roar of the surf from the Atlantic Ocean. She wouldn't be able to tell weather conditions solely by the force of the waves hitting shore. She'd not be able to wade along the tide line, nor would she be able to wander freely as she did now.

She had Jacob to thank for that. His presence allowed her to remain where she wanted to be. She turned her attention to the man at her side. She wished she could see him more clearly. As it was, the sun silhouetted his broad shoulders, and she could tell he wasn't the skinny boy who'd left her behind. She wondered how the planes of his face had changed with the years. She felt sure her vision would clear again. She'd see him soon enough. And even if she didn't, she had the details of the past tucked away in her memory. His sea green eyes wouldn't have changed, but his hair apparently had. Judging by the way the strands blew around in the wind, he'd let it grow longer than before, but she imagined the strands were the same sun-kissed color they used to be. He never had been one to stay indoors any more than necessary.

Her uncle's voice intruded on her musings. "I think we're ready. We need to finish up and be on our way." The usually wordy man surprised her as he made quick work of the ceremony.

"Jacob, you may now kiss your bride."

Before Hollan could work up a full panic, Jacob leaned forward and gently touched his lips to hers in the most gentle of kisses. Against her will, her heart began to soar.

❧

The first few days of their marriage were awkward to say the least. Jacob could see the strain as Hollan tried to work into a steady routine of normalcy. They started each day with breakfast. Hollan worked hard to have the meal on the table before he arrived at the cottage door.

"You aren't normally an early riser, are you?" Jacob asked

during their meal on their fourth morning together.

"Why do you ask?" she questioned, hiding a yawn behind her hand.

He laughed. "You're about to fall asleep in your eggs. At first I figured you weren't sleeping well due to our new role as—neighbors."

"We aren't simple neighbors, and you know it." She swiped his half-eaten plate of food from in front of him and made her way to the counter. "We're in a completely unique situation, and I do find myself losing sleep trying to make sense of it all." She snatched up a rag and returned to the table, wiping hard at the crumbs.

"You trying to wipe clean through the wood?" He stayed her hand with his.

Her breathing hitched, and she quickly pulled away. "Don't you have a lighthouse to tend to?"

"Again the lack of subtlety." He enjoyed putting a blush on her cheeks. He stood and pushed in his chair. "But yes, I do need to wipe down the lens."

"Don't forget to trim the wicks. And refuel the lanterns."

"Did all that before coming in for breakfast. Some of us get up early."

"Or never go to bed at all," she muttered.

"I sleep. I just don't need a lot of it. I sneak in a few hours before dusk and in between work."

Hollan rolled her eyes.

"Let me know if you need me." He wondered if she'd ever truly need him. If she'd ever care about him the way she used to.

He closed the cottage door behind him and walked over to the lighthouse. He climbed the multitude of narrow stairs that led to the top level. The day was clear, and he could see a good ways out. As had become his habit, he went around the entire walkway, looking for any sign of Hollan's father. If the man hadn't washed out to sea, he didn't know what had happened to him. For Hollan's sake, he hoped they'd someday find out. Hollan told him the lighthouse inspector was due for a visit within the month, and if her father hadn't returned, they stood to lose the contract. In the meantime, he'd do everything he could to keep the light in good working order.

Jacob slipped into Hollan's father's cleaning coat. The lens had to be immaculate at all times in order to work properly. He first wiped away all loose particles of debris with a feather duster. He then used a fine cloth to carefully remove any smudges left by the oil. The prisms were delicate and easily scratched, so he always made sure to touch them with caution.

He spent longer than he'd intended on the job, and the sun tipped slightly toward the west before he headed to the cottage for the midday meal. Hollan waited in a chair out front, staring toward the horizon, her forehead creased with concern.

"Is something wrong?"

"It's getting ready to storm." She motioned toward a cloth-covered plate that sat on a small table tucked between the two chairs. Samson lifted his tawny head and wagged his tail in acknowledgment before lowering his chin back down to rest upon his front paws, his favorite napping position.

Jacob surveyed the horizon. He saw some dark clouds, but he knew Hollan and her father recognized the signs of a serious storm much better than he. "Will it be a bad one?"

"I'm not sure." She'd balled her handkerchief into a small mass. "I just know the weather's turned. The seagulls have taken refuge."

He hadn't noticed, but now that she mentioned it, the ever-present birds weren't anywhere around.

"Tell me what I need to do." He didn't bother with his plate.

She smiled, but the lines around her mouth betrayed her tension. "First of all, eat. If it's a big storm, you'll be busy later."

"Then talk to me while I eat." He lifted his plate onto his lap and took a bite of crab cake. It was delicately seasoned and cooked to perfection. She'd garnished the plate with a side of tomato that he'd picked fresh from her garden earlier in the day. "This crab cake is wonderful. The tomato looks good, too."

"Thank you," she said absently. Not one to be easily distracted when she had her mind set on something, she continued to stare toward the horizon. "Do you see any clouds?"

He glanced at the ocean as he took a sip of water. "There's a darkening of the sky way out, but otherwise it's blue."

"The storms move in quickly. We'll need to batten down everything we can. The chairs and table need to go in the storage building, along with anything loose. I'm sure the process is the same as the one you'd go through in town."

"You're thinking this will be a large storm?"

"According to the birds, yes. But we won't know how large till it hits."

For the first time, he saw a chink in her armor. She'd been great about their whole situation, but her nervousness over the storm's approach was palpable. He reached over and clasped her hand with his. "God is sufficient for all our needs, Hollan. Always remember that. We'll be fine."

She didn't look convinced. "I've lost both my mother and my father in storms. They'll never be my favorite thing."

"That's understandable."

The wind picked up. The cloth that had covered his plate blew off the table, and Jacob jumped up to chase it. He glanced back at the horizon and saw the churning clouds moving closer at a quick pace.

"It's coming," Hollan stated.

"Yes." He gathered the plate and his mug and carried them into the house. He returned for Hollan. "Come. You'll be more comfortable inside."

Hollan shook her head. "I'll help with the preparations. Do you need to do anything with the light? It'll be needed more than ever during the storm."

"I have everything ready."

They worked around the yard, stowing any loose gardening gear in the storage building. The sky darkened. Clouds passed over the cottage and covered the sun. Hollan shivered.

"I need to light the lanterns. Let me see you into the house."

"I'd like to wait out here if you don't mind. I'll move in before things get rough."

"As you wish. But I'd feel better if you waited inside."

"Will you wait out the storm in the lighthouse? Or would you"—she hesitated—"consider waiting it out with me?"

"I'll be back as soon as my duties are taken care of."

Relief flowed across her pretty features. "Thank you." She waved him away.

He hurried through the motions of lighting the wicks that he'd already trimmed to the perfect length. He'd need to return in about four hours to trim them again, but as he looked around everything else was in order. The rain had begun a few minutes earlier, but now it came down in earnest. His cozy room waiting below beckoned him—he'd be drenched before he ever reached Hollan—but he'd given her his word. He didn't want her sitting through the storm alone, frightened.

He'd just exited the door at the base of the lighthouse, when a gust of wind slammed it shut behind him. The wind pushed him along as he moved toward the cottage. Hollan waited in the doorway, anxiety written across her face.

"I'm here, Hollan. I'm coming. Stay put."

Samson heard Jacob and shoved his way through the narrow opening, knocking Hollan off balance.

"Samson, no!" Hollan lunged for the escaping dog. She struggled to retain her balance against the force of the storm, but the wind caught her skirts and twirled them in a tangle around her legs. Before Jacob could get to her, she fell, tumbling down the steps with a scream. Her head hit the stone walkway, and she lay unmoving in a crumpled heap.

six

Samson turned at once, hurrying back to his mistress. Jacob pushed him aside and scooped Hollan up in his arms.

"C'mon, Samson, let's get her inside." Rain blew through the open doorway as Jacob entered. He hurried to deposit Hollan on the quilt-covered bed. He forced the door shut before turning to stoke the fire. Though the fire burned warm, the light wasn't bright enough for him to check Hollan for injuries.

He lit a lamp and placed it on a small table near the bed. Samson, panting, stood with his front paws on the edge of the bed. He whined and licked Hollan's hand.

"She'll be fine." Jacob hoped his words were the truth.

The dog looked unconvinced.

"Hollan, can you hear me?" Jacob caressed Hollan's cheek with the back of his hand.

She remained still, her skin pale against the bright pastels of the quilt. He'd give anything to see her brown eyes open to peer into his. A trickle of blood ran down the side of her cheek. With careful fingers, Jacob tenderly sifted through her hair until he found the wound. It didn't appear to be deep at first glance, but with the amount of blood loss, it needed his attention.

First, though, he had to get her out of her wet shoes and dress. "Samson, help me out here. Hollan will tan my hide if she thinks I took any liberties with her."

Samson turned tail and headed for the fire, though he did thump his tail three times in sympathy before curling up into

48

a cozy ball. Or at least Jacob imagined the thumps were a show of sympathy.

"She's my wife, buddy. It's fine, really."

Then why, he asked himself, *am I talking to the dog like he can understand or even cares about my justification of what I'm about to do?*

"She'll get pneumonia if she continues to lie here in a wet dress."

Samson snorted, and Jacob figured it was the dog's way of laughing at his dilemma. Or maybe the sound was just a contented sigh because as a dog Samson didn't have to worry about such things. Or maybe it was just a random dog sound that had nothing at all to do with the crazy individual who was talking to him, trying to figure out the inner workings of a dog's brain when he really needed to be caring for the woman who lay helpless in front of him.

Jacob decided to ignore the irritating thoughts that were pummeling through his head, and with purpose he unhooked Hollan's boots and slipped them off her slender feet. Though he knew she hated it, she'd taken to wearing the boots ever since she cut her foot on the shell. He doubted the habit would continue after she healed.

Next his clumsy fingers unfastened enough tiny buttons down the front of her dress to rival the amount of stairs in the lighthouse before he was finally able to pull the wet material down and over Hollan's arms. He tugged it down over her waist and away from her motionless body. He was relieved to find her underclothes dry, so he was able to leave her covered. Her petticoat and camisole did a fine job of keeping her modesty intact. He did a cursory examination for further injuries before tucking the blankets around her. He slipped the wet quilt from the bed and with a sigh of relief that the deed was done, moved the quilt and the dress nearer to the fire to dry.

Jacob dipped some warm water from the pot that hung over the flame into a small bowl. A huge gust of wind blowing against the cottage made him jump. The storm was intensifying. It sounded like this one might turn into a full-fledged hurricane. At least in her present state, Hollan wouldn't worry about their safety.

The search for rags took a bit longer, but soon he was back at Hollan's side, ready to clean her wound. He said a quick prayer of thanks that he hadn't seen any other signs of injury while he settled her in. He could only pray the head wound wasn't as bad as it looked.

"It's already stopped bleeding, Samson. That's a good sign, don't you think?"

This time Samson didn't even bother to open an eye. Jacob found it reassuring that the dog didn't seem nervous about the storm.

"I'll take that as a sign that you trust she's in good hands," Jacob muttered as he cleaned the wound. Now that the bleeding had stopped, the cut didn't appear to be deep at all.

A lump was forming under the gash. Jacob was cautious as he smoothed Hollan's auburn hair away from her face. Even now she was so beautiful. "You're going to be all right, Hollan. I'm here with you."

He couldn't do anything more for her for the time being. He slipped into some of her father's dry clothes that he had found in a trunk across the room and hung his own clothes to dry. He finally settled in a chair beside Hollan's bed and began to pray.

❧

Hollan opened her eyes and peered into the dusky gloom. The effort was rewarded by a shooting pain that forced her to close them again. She struggled to get her bearings. She remembered the storm and Samson slipping past her. She'd reached for him and had fallen. She had no memory beyond that, except for waking in the bed minutes earlier.

I hope the injury didn't affect my returning vision. Slowly, realization flowed over her. She'd opened her eyes and had *seen* into the gloom. She'd been able to see perfectly. The few images she'd been able to take in were engraved upon her mind. The fire burned low. Samson slept near the hearth, closer than was safe, as usual. Her dress and a quilt, along with a set of men's clothes, hung on the backs of chairs near the fire to dry.

Men's clothes hung by the fire? She noticed the sound of deep breathing from a chair pulled up close beside her. She opened her eyes again, slower this time to let her eyes acclimate, and for the first time in three years she stared fully into the handsome face of the man she'd once loved. Jacob was stronger, sturdier, but still as striking as ever.

"Jacob." She whispered the word softly, but his eyes flew open as soon as she uttered it.

"Hollan." He slipped from the chair and onto his knees beside her. "How do you feel?"

She couldn't stop looking at him. "Dizzy."

"You hit your head pretty good right about here." He touched his fingers near the wound then caressed lightly down her temple. "You gave Samson and me quite a scare."

"I'm sorry." She shivered at his touch. To cover her reaction, she reached up and felt the raised bump.

"I hardly think you meant to do it." He pulled her hand away from the wound and smiled. "I cleaned the injury, but you'll want to be careful. It will be tender for a few days."

"Thank you." She peered over his shoulder. He didn't release her hand. He was too close. She felt vulnerable. "Has the storm passed?"

"Not completely, but it has calmed down some."

Her head ached. She closed her eyes and listened to the rain pattering against the roof. The aroma of simmering stew set her mouth to watering. And Jacob hovered nearby. The thought made her tremble.

"You're shivering. Let me stoke the fire."

It wasn't the cold that caused her tremor. She felt plenty warm in the cocoon of blankets he'd apparently tucked around her. It was his gentle touch that made her shiver, that stoked a whole other fire and set forth a new longing within her, a longing for things to be as they had been before. Back when he wanted to marry her out of love, not obligation. Before he left town, before she'd lost her sight, and before she'd lost her parents.

She studied him as he moved about the hearth, stepping carefully over the sleeping dog. His hair was indeed longer. He'd pulled it away from his face, which accentuated his high cheekbones. He smiled as he worked, his features relaxed with relief. When he leaned in from the far side, the fire flared, and she could see the green of the eyes she'd missed looking into for so long.

A sudden panic ran through her. Her vision felt different this time. It felt permanent. She couldn't put her finger on the change, but she had peace that her vision would remain. What if, now that she could see again, Jacob decided she no longer needed him and he was free to move on? He could have their marriage annulled and return to his previous plans—whatever those plans might have been. Surely he had some. She wasn't ready for more changes. Not yet anyway.

"What are you thinking?"

Hollan jumped. She hadn't noticed him crossing the floor to her side.

"Tell me your thoughts. You looked scared there for a

moment." He pulled his chair closer and settled beside her. "Whatever your concerns were, don't worry about a thing. I'm here, and I don't intend to leave."

So you say now. When you find out you don't have to watch out for me anymore, you might feel differently.

She so badly wanted to stare into his eyes. Instead she closed her own and feigned weariness. "If you don't mind, then, I'll rest for a little bit longer."

"Do you really want to sleep, or are you merely avoiding the truth?"

"The truth?" Did he still know her so well after all these years? Had he noticed the change in her as she savored the familiar sight of his face?

"I think I understand. You're uncomfortable with our arrangement, yet you fear being alone. I'm sure this isn't easy for you."

So he didn't know her vision had fully returned. If she kept it that way a bit longer—at least until she had her bearings about her and could come up with a new plan—it would give her more time to think things through. Her head hurt and everything felt too overwhelming. She'd be able to make better decisions in the next few days.

"I feared being alone through the storm far more than I fear your closeness." There. She'd said it. But she wasn't sure that was completely true. His presence brought about a sense of awareness and accentuated an emptiness she hadn't noticed before he'd arrived back on the island. Already his presence brought her a sense of peace that she didn't want to lose. The fear of losing him so soon rivaled the fear of the storm. "At least, for the moment I *think* that's true." She cringed. She should probably stop talking until she had more rest and could think through her words, *before* stating them, with a clear mind.

He leaned close, his lips near her ear, causing tiny bumps to rise up on her forearms. "My closeness makes you nervous?"

She ordered her eyes to remain closed, though she longed to open them and see his face. She could feel the warmth of his breath on her skin.

"Yes," she admitted through clenched teeth. The man was toying with her. She didn't feel as bad about keeping her returned vision a secret at this rate. Here she lay helpless in bed and he used the situation to his advantage. She held back her smile. Deep down she didn't really mind his teasing.

Now he raised a finger and caressed her cheek. His touch was so gentle, so considerate; the act caused tears to form in her eyes. Her emotions were all over the place.

She opened her eyes. "I have a confession to make. My vision comes and goes. For the moment my vision has returned."

His face lit up. "That's wonderful news!"

"It is, but I'm confused and overwhelmed." And that was the pure truth. Hollan hadn't felt so mixed up and inundated with changes since she'd lost her mother.

"Have you prayed about it?"

She released a small breath and stared at the beams that ran across the ceiling. "I haven't prayed about much of anything in a long, long time."

"You don't believe anymore? You've lost your faith?"

The disappointment and concern in his voice had her firing off the first answer that came to mind. "No!"

She hesitated before saying anything more and analyzed his question a bit more thoroughly. *Had* she lost her faith? At the very least, she'd buried it beneath the pile of rubble that had been her former life.

"I'm embarrassed to say I haven't given it much thought lately." Guilt pricked at her conscience. If her faith had been strong, would she have let it drift away so easily? Most people used their faith to get them through the tough times—they didn't forget about it completely. "What does that say about me?"

"It says you've been through a lot." He shifted his position. "Is God still in charge of your life?"

"I guess so. . . I mean, yes, I want Him to be. I haven't given it much thought before now."

"God understands anger. But you can't let the anger make you so bitter that you turn against Him."

"No, of course not. Yet that seems to be exactly what I've done. That night. . .I lost so much."

"I know what you lost." Jacob tightened his grip on her hand. "Do you want to tell me about it? I feel responsible."

"How could you be responsible when you weren't even here?" She hadn't meant the words to sound so venomous. It might help to talk about it, to share with Jacob what happened that night. "Mama and I were talking about the wedding when we heard a noise outside. Mama went to check. A storm lurked over the water, and the wind had started up. I stayed inside and continued to work on our dinner, and the next thing I knew, Papa came in through the door. He said he'd sent Mama inside."

She untwisted and smoothed the sheets she'd wrung tight with her hands. He reached over and massaged away the tension that had gathered in her clenched hands. His touch encouraged her to continue. He deserved to know. The experiences had shaped her into the person she was today.

"Mama hadn't returned, and we both knew something wasn't right. Papa was upset and ran to check the beach while I searched the grounds around the house. Neither one of us thought to check the lighthouse, because Papa had just come from there. After looking out over the dune, I turned to go back to the house and I saw a flash of color from the ledge that circles the light. Papa couldn't hear me, so I went up without him. Mama had been crying, and she stood at the rail, much too close to the edge with the storm brewing around us."

Her breath hitched.

Jacob wiped away a tear she hadn't realized she'd shed. "Maybe now isn't the best time. You need to rest, not get more upset."

His voice was husky, full of emotion, and she wondered at the remorse she heard in his tone.

"No, I need to do this." She took a deep breath. "I went out there, and the wind buffeted around me. It almost blew me over the edge. My mother didn't even acknowledge my presence. I called to her and tried to pull her back inside, but she shoved me away. I fell against the stone wall and hit my head. When I came to, I'd lost my sight and Mama all in one fell swoop. Papa saw us up there, but before he could get to the top, Mama had jumped."

"No one knows why?"

"No, we never found out. She took her secret to the grave." Her voice had dropped to a whisper, but now she laughed, the sound harsh in the silence. "What kind of mother does that to her child—even if the child is almost grown? What type of wife abandons her husband in such a painful way? How could she have done that to herself and to us?"

"Hollan, maybe she didn't jump. If the wind was that strong, maybe she fell over accidently."

"Why was she up there?"

"I don't have the answers to those questions, Hollan. I wish I did."

Hollan understood his confusion.

"I know. I don't really expect you to. But therein lies the reason for my silence and distance from God. It wasn't a conscious choice I made, but I stopped communicating with Him." She hesitated. "I haven't forgotten my father's and uncle's teachings. I've even talked to God a bit lately. But still I've drifted away."

"Now that you've realized this, are you ready to make things right with Him?"

She nodded. "I am. I want to find my way back."

"He'll calm your fears and will help you sort through all the changes you're experiencing." He chuckled. "Changes we're both going through. If we work as a team, perhaps we can make sense of it all and see what God has for us. Let me pray with you."

Jacob clasped her hand and leaned forward to rest his forehead against it. She clung to him like the lifeline he was. The strength and confidence in his warm voice as he prayed washed over her.

"Lord, we join together in prayer and thank You for keeping us safe through the storm. Help Hollan back into the fold, Lord, and use me to make the process easier. We ask that You bring Hollan clarity of mind and calm her fears in all situations. She wants You to take control of her life. Guide her in all things. . . . In Jesus' name, amen."

Hollan listened as he finished up his prayer and felt a sense of peace flow through her. She released to Him all the fears and concerns she'd carried. For the first time in a while, she felt the burdens she'd carried alone lift. She held only one small concern back for herself. She knew she was supposed to turn *everything* over to God, to let Him watch over all aspects of her life, but in this one small area she still felt she needed to keep control, at least for a little bit longer. For now, for just a little bit longer, she still felt the need to keep the permanent return of her vision a secret from Jacob.

seven

After two days in bed, Hollan couldn't wait any longer to get out and explore the island. She understood Jacob's over-protective nature after a blow to her head, but she wanted to get up. She had a lot to celebrate. Her *vision* had returned! It hadn't wavered once. She sent a covert glance at Jacob. And neither had the man she still loved. He'd returned and now stayed close to her side. But that all-important detail aside, at the moment she only wanted to see the places and things she loved through new eyes. And even better would be to see everything with Jacob by her side.

"We're going out to explore today." Hollan settled at the table, not leaving her comment up for debate. "I feel completely ready to go outside and breathe in some fresh air. If I have to stay inside another day, I'll surely go insane."

"You will, huh?" Jacob set an aromatic plate of eggs in front of her before taking his seat. "We certainly don't want that. A little fresh air won't hurt, but you'll need to take it slow."

"Yes, doc." She busied herself with eating, not wanting to waste a moment of the brilliant day that waited outside their doorstep. "Jacob, these eggs are wonderful. Where'd you learn to cook like this?"

"All over the place." He stabbed at an egg, and she took the moment to study him. His damp hair was slicked back from his forehead. "When you travel like I did, you meet up with a lot of different people. I had to work a lot of odd jobs in order to make ends meet."

"How did you end up choosing to do that? What made

you decide to become a traveling preacher? I don't remember you ever talking about wanting to do such a thing."

What she really wanted to ask was why he'd left her behind. From the way he froze in place, fork halfway to his mouth while contemplating his answer, she knew she'd hit a sore spot.

"That night I left, a lot of bad things happened." He laid his fork down and reached over to toy with her hand. She had a hard time not staring into his eyes. She wanted to lose herself in them. But he couldn't know about the return of her vision. Not yet. She didn't want him to leave. She wasn't ready for that possibility. She needed more time. She needed to solidify their relationship.

"I remember."

"I know you do." He pulled his hand away and ran it through his hair, the gesture reassuringly familiar. "I couldn't face anyone after what my father and brothers did to the people of our town. So when they fled, I chased them up the trail. They scattered, and I tailed them one at a time. Each time I'd catch one, I turned him over to the law." He picked up his fork and used it to push the eggs back and forth, but he didn't eat any of them.

"That had to be hard." Hollan ached for him, for the pain he had to have felt each time he had to turn in a brother. "You found your father, too?"

"Someone else found him first. I found his body soon after."

"That's awful." What else could she say to that? Though she longed to know what had happened to her father, finding his body wasn't something she could imagine. She didn't want to contemplate it further. "And the others, what happened to them?"

"I found all but one. They'll spend a lot of time behind bars, if not worse. I didn't stick around to see what happened."

"Which one evaded you?"

"David."

He seemed to be studying her face for a reaction. She stared at his chin. His expression turned quizzical when she didn't have one.

"So you decided to let him go, and instead you returned home?"

"No, I trailed him back this way. I don't intend to stop looking until he joins our other brothers behind bars."

"So you're only here for a short while?"

"I married you, Hollan. I'm with you for life. I meant my vows when I said them."

Her heart leaped at his words. Maybe she wouldn't have to keep her secret as long as she thought. She tested him.

"But you were forced into the marriage. You might change your mind if. . ." She let her voice trail off, not sure what to say.

"If what?" His voice held a chuckle. "I made my commitment for life, Hollan."

He stood to gather their plates and moved out of her line of vision. Her *newly returned* vision. A hint of a smile broadened her lips. She savored the thought and forced herself not to track him with her eyes.

"Well, I don't know. What if you get bored? What if you catch your brother and want to travel again? I understand you wanted to return home and right the wrongs of your family, but once that's all behind you, maybe you'll want to wander again."

"Not likely." This time there was no humor after the statement. "A person can only wander for so long before life catches up with them. And in my case, it was time for me to return."

"So what about David?"

He helped her up from her chair and led the way to the door. "I'll know what to do when the time comes. God has led me to each of them in turn. I don't know why David came back. He already caused all the pain he possibly could. But for whatever reason, God has been urging me back this way for a while now, and I've ignored Him. Next thing I know, my quarry turned this way and led me home."

"Interesting." Hollan wished he'd come back because he missed her. But they were married and working on their new relationship. That had to be enough. She'd try to be patient and see what happened next.

"Enough of that. Let's go explore and see what the hurricane did to our home."

Our home. The words were so simple, yet they meant so much to her. She wasn't alone anymore.

Jacob tugged her toward the inland channel. "How about we start at the dock? I want to check the boat."

Hollan nodded her agreement.

Jacob led her down the path toward the water at a leisurely pace, walking slightly ahead. She held back just a bit, wanting to look around without him taking notice. She savored every single sight. The brilliant green of the trees stood out against the vivid blue of the sky. The seagulls circled overhead, scavenging for small crabs and fish. They neared the sandy beach, and the water lapped at the shore, tossing tiny shells and clams with the movement. The sea oats danced in the slight breeze. Hollan wanted to dance along with them. Pelicans and herons dove for their dinner in the distance. And decidedly the best view of all was that of Jacob walking just ahead of her. Her beloved Jacob. She studied his broad shoulders and the way his waist narrowed at the hips. The muscles in his arms flexed as he cleared debris from their path. The sun shone off his golden hair, which he'd again pulled back and tied at the nape of his neck. He was truly a striking man.

Jacob's grunt pulled her from her perusal. He'd stopped just ahead of her. She wanted to wrap her arms around him and press her cheek against his back, but instead she hurried to stand at his side. She glanced at the dock.

Only one thing seemed to be missing—one major thing. She put her hand to her forehead and scanned the open waters.

"The boat's gone." Jacob stated the obvious just before Hollan blurted it out. At the rate she was going, she'd surely clue him in about the return of her sight. Jacob didn't notice—he was too focused on the missing boat.

"Gone...where?"

Jacob reached over to clutch her hand. "I have no idea. I didn't think the storm would have done that much damage to this side of the island. It's more protected."

"Odd."

"Yes, it is." His voice held a funny tone.

"Are you thinking someone tampered with it?"

"I'm not sure. But it can't have floated off on its own."

"The supply boat won't be here for days. This means we're on our own until then."

"It looks that way." They'd reached the dock, and Jacob released her hand as he bent low to check out the dock and surrounding water. He stood back up, hands on hips, and glanced around again. "This is so strange. There's no sign of it at all."

"The storm likely blew it away. I doubt we'll ever find it."

"What now?"

"There's nothing we can do until Fletcher returns."

He clasped her hand again and led her down the shoreline

path. His hand felt solid and reassuring. "Let's walk some more. Maybe it washed ashore. If so, we'll come across it. If not, I still want to see what other damage the storm did to our island."

They walked in silence, and more than once Hollan's eyes blurred with tears of happiness. A lizard skittered across the path and disappeared in the overgrown foliage to her left. A large turtle floated in the water just offshore. The water was so clear here that she could see the turtle's shadow on the sandy bottom as it moved along. A mockingbird sang from somewhere in the dense trees overhead. She'd missed these sights dearly. And because she never dared to walk very far, she'd missed a lot of the shoreline's sounds. Hollan took a deep breath, breathing in the salt-laden air. The vivid blue of the sky almost hurt her eyes, but she embraced the sensation. She'd never been happier to squint.

Jacob slowed. "Where does that path lead? I've never noticed it before."

"What path?"

Jacob tugged her inland, a small path barely visible through the dense jungle of palmettos and scrub that made most of the island impenetrable. "It leads through the undergrowth. It looks like at one time it would have been used quite often, but now it's almost completely overgrown."

"Sounds like the path to Amos's old place." Hollan was beginning to hate the farce she'd put into motion. If only she had complete surety that the return of her vision wouldn't cause a negative change in their budding friendship.

"Amos?" Jacob took the lead through the tunnel of vegetation. Hollan's skirts were snagged and tugged by the ends of the palmettos' sharp fronds. She didn't care. She'd happily sacrifice the old dress she wore for the experience and adventure of refamiliarizing herself with the interior of the island. Especially when it meant Jacob would hold her close against his side as he did now.

"He helped my grandfather when he first took over the lighthouse, before my father had the contract. He had a small shack somewhere around here."

"Let's find it."

"If it's even standing." She laughed. "It's been around for a long time, and you know how harsh the weather can be."

"It's still here."

Sure enough, it was. And it looked surprisingly solid. Of course she couldn't admit that to him.

The door screeched as he pulled it open. Hollan screamed as a bat flew out, barely skimming her head.

"Sorry about that." Jacob pulled her into a quick embrace. "It's gone now."

Hollan shuddered. She'd never liked the creatures of the night. Suddenly the area felt dark and oppressive. She couldn't imagine how much worse it would be if she couldn't see. Snakes loved to lurk on this section of the island, along with alligators and all sorts of other creatures.

"If you've seen enough, I'm ready to go back to the shore."

"No, actually, I want to look a little closer. Other than the bats—"

"Plural? I thought there was only one!" Hollan reached up and scrubbed at her hair with both hands. "They're gone, aren't they?" She spun in a circle.

"They all flew away. You're fine." She didn't comment on the chuckle she heard in his tone. He stood in the open doorway. "But it looks like someone has been here recently. The interior isn't as rough as I'd expect after all these years."

Hollan stepped closer and grabbed hold of Jacob's arm. "Someone or—something?"

"Someone. The floor is cleared, and there's a sign of fire.

Let me duck inside."

"All the more reason to leave."

"I'll only be a moment."

"You do know there are snakes and gators around here? Don't leave me for long."

Hollan hugged her arms around her waist and scoured the area for signs of predators. A bubbling stream ran along the opposite side of the small clearing. Though she much preferred being outside in the open rather than being inside the tiny bat-infested cabin, her mind was quickly conjuring up quite a few alarming scenarios of possible creatures lurking at her feet.

"Um, Jacob? I'm hearing scurrying sounds in the brush. Not something I like to stand here and listen to. My imagination's racing out here."

"I'm ready." His sudden appearance at her side made her jump. "Let's get you out of here. But I'll be watching the place, and if someone is using this cabin, I'll find out."

"Sounds good to me. Meanwhile, I'll stick to waiting on one of the nice, clean, wide-open paths on the beach when you check."

Jacob laughed.

They cut across the island toward the ocean and reached the main path. Hollan breathed a sigh of relief. The sigh ended in a cough as she inhaled the sharp odor of rotting fish. Quite a few of them lay scattered at their feet. "Whoa. Lots of fish washed ashore in this area after the storm."

Jacob turned her way, eyes squinting, his forehead creased. Hollan covered quickly, waving her hand in front of her wrinkled nose.

He laughed. "It *is* a bit potent."

"It's the aroma of home. I like it."

"You are an island girl through and through, aren't you?"

"Always and forever." Hollan couldn't imagine living anywhere else. She didn't want to *think* about living anywhere else.

"Hollan, there's something we need to talk about."

Her heart plummeted. Here it came. She didn't want to hear what he had to say. "Oh listen! The waves are louder and the birds more vocal. We're nearing the ocean side, aren't we?"

"Yes." He squeezed her hand. "Hollan, don't change the subject."

Intent on savoring the newest view, she didn't answer. The Atlantic Ocean seemed to stretch out forever before her. Shells scattered at her feet, begging for her attention. She loved walking with Jacob, but she couldn't wait to make her escape in the near future and spend a morning enjoying her favorite pastime, looking for seashells and pirate treasure.

"Hollan?"

"I'm sorry." She kept her gaze down and moved forward.

"Anyway, as I was saying, we have to discuss what will happen if the lighthouse inspector arrives and decides that we can't stay."

She froze. "Decides we can't stay? Why would he decide that?" The panic made her voice rise. She hadn't even thought about that possibility.

"The contract for the lighthouse is with your father, not with us. I don't know how that all works, but he might have someone else in mind to take over for your father—now that he is missing."

"Well, he can just wait." She set her jaw, daring him to disagree. "We have no—*proof* that my father isn't coming back. Until we do, we need to protect his job."

"You have a point. We'll keep that as our plan for now." He gently guided her face to look up into his. "But you have to keep in mind that we might need an alternate plan."

Hollan carefully avoided his gaze after one quick glimpse of his beautiful green eyes. She had to end this farce—tomorrow. She wanted one more day to savor the sights and Jacob's presence before telling him how drastically things had changed. He seemed genuine in his commitment, but he didn't have all the facts. "There'll be no plan other than the one that allows us to stay on this island."

"As you wish." He smirked. "I suppose we can always move into Amos's place. Quarters might be tight, but I think we could make do. I certainly could."

Hollan stared straight ahead, but she felt the flush wash over her features. *Close quarters* would be an understatement. "There would be bugs and snakes and other equally horrible things. I couldn't even imagine."

"I'd batten it down. I'll make sure they don't get you."

"We'd have no beds. We'd have to—" The blush continued. "We'd have no room to move around."

"I'd hold you close and keep you safe."

Hollan didn't know what to say to that. She'd love to have him hold her close at night and keep her safe. But she wasn't sure she was ready for all the changes that would bring to their relationship. They were married after all, but she hadn't kept up with all the changes as it was. She needed them to take things slow. But he'd slept inside the cottage—albeit in a chair—for the past three nights. He'd watched over her since the hurricane. She didn't want to send him back to the lighthouse now.

"That might be—tolerable."

"Tolerable?" He choked on a laugh, his profile showing his dimples.

She shrugged. "I'd do my best to adapt."

"Tell me, which part might be merely tolerable? Living in the cabin?" He stepped close behind her and whispered in her ear. "Or being held in my arms at night?"

Hollan shivered. "If necessity mandated such a situation, I'd probably survive both conditions."

"You'd *probably* survive them?" Jacob laughed out loud. "That's nice to know."

He spun her around and pulled her close. She knew he was going to kiss her. She closed her eyes. He planted several soft kisses on her lips, and she felt herself respond and kiss him back.

"I've missed you, Hollan."

She asked the question that had bothered her for so long. "Then why'd you leave?"

"It's complicated. But my decision to leave that night had nothing to do with my feelings for you. My love for you has never changed."

Hollan's heart swelled. "I'm glad to know that."

"I'd like to tell you about it soon."

"Maybe tonight at dinner?"

"I don't know. You've had a busy morning, and I want you to rest. I think we need to get lunch, you need to lie down, and we'll see what the evening brings later."

"You're avoiding me."

"I wouldn't say I'm avoiding you exactly. . . . I'm just trying to give you the time to heal. Besides your head injury, you've lost your father. I want to take things slow. We have our whole life ahead of us, and there's no reason to hurry while we're muddling through all the changes."

"I have faith that my father is alive. My head injury is fine." Hollan's good spirits began to slip away. He was echoing her thoughts from a moment earlier that they needed to take things slow, yet now she found herself pushing forward. "When you use the word *muddling* as you just did, it feels as if you think you're stuck here in this awful. . .*quagmire*. . .or something with me."

"I'm not *stuck* in anything with you, Hollan, and I'm sorry if it came across that way." She leaned against his chest, and he rested his chin on her head. "I know I'm where God led me to be. I'm perfectly content to be where I am. I love being married to you, and I can only hope that in a very short time we'll be living as a married couple in every way."

"Then why—?"

"I won't take advantage of you in a vulnerable state. I want to make sure you're coming to me freely when we make this marriage real. I'll sleep in the lighthouse for tonight, and we'll see what tomorrow brings—tomorrow."

Disappointment rolled over Hollan, but she knew he was right. They'd work things out as they went. But she knew she'd miss his presence in the cottage tonight.

They circled around toward the dunes in front of their home, and Jacob led her directly toward a piece of driftwood. She panicked. If she stepped over it, he'd know. If she had to trip, she'd feel like an idiot. It served her right for her deceit.

She slowed just as she reached the limb and bent down to fumble with her boot.

"Is everything all right?"

"Everything is fine, thank you."

"So we can continue on?"

"Yes."

At that slower pace, she had no trouble kicking her foot toward the driftwood. Jacob stopped her.

"There's a piece of wood in front of us. Come this way, and we'll go around it."

"Thanks," she mumbled.

"We need to head up to the cottage."

"Let's keep going." Hollan wanted to see it all. Everything she'd missed seeing for the past three years.

"No. You need to get back and rest. And I need to check the lighthouse."

When she started to protest, he put a finger against her lips.

"You suffered a huge blow to the head. I don't want you to overtax yourself. We'll walk the other way in the morning." They continued in the direction of the dunes. "If you want us to save our post, we need to be ready and have things perfect at any given time."

"Good point." She sighed. "I'll come up with you." She couldn't wait to see the view from atop the lighthouse!

"You'll return to the cottage and sleep."

She made a disgruntled sound, and Jacob laughed. "You'll be up to par soon enough, wife. You need to have patience."

Wife. She grinned. "I'm up to par now. My tyrant of a husband just won't let me prove it."

Silence met her hasty retort, and she wondered if she had inadvertently offended him. Instead her eyes widened as Jacob leaned in for another gentle kiss. "I'm sure you have a lot to prove, wife, and I anticipate and look forward to each and every revelation."

He accentuated the word *revelation*. Was he insinuating something? Her guilt had her constantly returning to her deception. She stubbornly stood her ground. She liked things as they were. She didn't want to mess things up.

He captured her gaze with his own, and she swooned. She stepped backward. Jacob caught her by the arm. "Dizzy?"

"A—a bit maybe." She put a hand to her forehead and feigned exhaustion. No way would she admit that it was his kiss that threw her off balance. "I think you're right about my lying down."

"I'll get you settled then."

She ignored the laughter in his voice. She hadn't fooled him in the least.

eight

Hollan rose at dawn, determined to get an early start on her day. She figured the best way to effectively avoid Jacob would be to ease out the door well before their usual meeting time. He wouldn't be happy with her, but she needed some time alone. She wanted to be able to explore without hiding the fact that she could see. Today she'd tell him about the return of her vision—just as soon as she took this walk along the shore.

She had a feeling their relationship would take a turn for the better after she cleared the air. She looked forward to sharing her news. She hadn't liked sleeping alone in the cottage after having Jacob there the three nights before. She wanted their marriage to be real.

If Jacob felt she didn't need him anymore and he decided to move on, she'd work through the situation day by day, just as she'd dealt with every other challenge in her life. But she hoped and prayed he wouldn't decide that because she really did need him. She knew now that her love for him had never diminished; it had merely been buried somewhere deep inside.

Hollan stood before the mirror and smiled at her reflection. Today she could brush and style her auburn hair, and she would know what the end result actually looked like. She'd picked her favorite dress to wear and loved how the deep blue color she'd never seen before so perfectly matched the hue of the sea. Her brown eyes sparkled with excitement in the mirror's reflection. Soon she'd be walking along the beach, scouring the soft sand for shells. Seagulls called to her through the open cottage door. The waves pounded the shoreline in the distance, promising interesting treasure.

Mindful of the time, she hurried to prepare a batch of blueberry muffins. She arranged them on a plate and set a flowered bowl of butter and a matching one of jam beside them. Guilt had her scurrying to the garden for a pretty arrangement of flowers. Jacob likely wouldn't notice, but if he did, maybe he'd realize she'd taken the extra step to make her absence less harsh. Then again, he'd probably not even miss her and would be thrilled to have a morning meal without the awkwardness of their usual forced routine, though she had to admit their camaraderie felt more natural compared to before her accident. She now felt a certain comfort in the presence of her husband.

When she couldn't think of anything else to do, she hurried out the door. Samson tried to follow, but she knew his barking would draw Jacob's attention. She blocked him with her leg and forced the door shut behind her. The dog would get even by leading Jacob straight to her side but hopefully not before she'd had plenty of time to savor the beauty of her surroundings. And when they arrived, she'd happily share her news with Jacob, and she'd ask him to move into the cottage so they could properly live like the married couple they were.

Hollan wasted no time moving past the lighthouse and let out a sigh of relief after she'd cleared the stone walls. Once on the beach, she breathed even easier. No voice called out to stop her. No footsteps pounded down the hard-packed sand walkway in her wake.

Her bare feet sank deep into the coolness of the powdery soft sand at the water's edge, and she laughed out loud, wiggling her toes in order to bury them deeper. She wanted to do so many different things. She wanted to swim, to explore, and to merely sit and savor. But first she had to make haste and get far away from here. She followed the shore in the direction they'd been heading the previous day. A tide pool usually formed just around the curve of the farthest dune, and she hoped to find it alive with crawling creatures. While she didn't care for most of the land-type creatures, she loved each and every one of the aquatic types.

And suddenly there it was—the tide pool—spread out before her, sparkling in the morning sun. From a distance the tidal pool looked placid, just a thin layer of water filling up the slight depression in the sand. But Hollan knew it would contain a whole underwater world full of sea creatures. Smiling, she dropped to her knees on the dry sand and studied the undersea world before her. She'd often wished in the past, as a little girl, that she could shrink down and be able to swim with the inhabitants. Now she was content just to be able to watch the miniature world. Everything she could see was a blessing and a privilege. She'd never take her vision for granted again.

Tiny coquina clams waved their siphons around, waiting for algae or plankton, not knowing they were a target themselves for the scavenging seagulls that flew overhead. Hermit crabs, their shells shiny and multicolored, glistened as they scurried across the bottom of the pool. A small blue crab lurked behind a rounded rock. A group of tiny fish swam together, twisting and turning with perfect precision. The scent of sea blew in on the breeze.

Hollan moved her fingers through the surface of the water, smiling as the clams pulled their siphons under the sand. The blue crab disappeared from sight when her hand's shadow moved too close. The hermit crabs pulled back into their shells. The fish darted away to the far side of the pool.

Something brushed against her foot, and she looked over

to see a curious ghost crab hurrying away. It blended in with the color of the beach and disappeared down a tunnel dug into the sand nearby. She felt as if her favorite friends had all gathered to welcome her back. All these aquatic creatures she'd missed for so long. She sat and savored the sights.

Hollan settled onto her hip and curved her legs beneath her. She dug her fingers into the sand and let it sift through them as she breathed a heartfelt prayer of thanks for the return of her vision. She knew God had a purpose in returning her sight, but this moment defined why she personally valued the ability to see. Her entire world here at the beach revolved around the land and the creatures she loved so much.

She glanced up. Fluffy white clouds moved across the brilliant blue sky. The water wasn't quite as brown as it had been the day before. The sediment churned up by the storm was settling, allowing the water to return to its natural blue green color.

Hollan wished she could throw caution to the wind and run out into the waves. But she wouldn't. Jacob would probably be along soon, looking for his errant wife.

Instead she stood slowly to her feet and began to move farther down the beach. She stayed close to the waterline, not wanting to miss a treasure. Though most shells lay in pieces, tossed and broken by the surf, a few choice shells made it through the treacherous waters. One particularly delicate-looking shell washed up at her feet. The wave flipped it upside down to show a perfect outer shell, the color bleached white by the sun.

Hollan picked it up, feeling a strange kinship with the item. She'd add it to her collection. She tucked the shell into her pocket. Several starfish and sea horses had washed in, too. She carefully lifted them and settled them back in the water. Most floated atop the water and drifted out to sea. But a few gave halfhearted efforts to swim before seeming to realize they were once again free to swim away to safety.

She was fully absorbed in her observations of the sea life at her feet. Hollan didn't notice the arrival of a large ship until the sound of men's voices carried to her from across the water. She stood watching the activity aboard ship, deciding it was likely a renegade privateer ship from the war. She knew from her father that a select few still sailed up and down the coast. Fascinated, she raised her hand to her forehead, shading her eyes so she could study the magnificent vessel.

"What have we here, gentlemen?"

Hollan jumped and swung around as a voice spoke close behind her. The hair stood up on the back of her neck.

A rough-looking man stood just to her right, and a bit farther back three others stood and leered at her. None of them looked like gentlemen as far as she was concerned.

She slowly backed away. She hadn't heard the arrival of the small boat that was now pulled up behind her down the shore. A shiver passed through her. For the first time that day, she prayed for Jacob to hurry and find her.

"I think we have a damsel in distress," one of the men muttered. "We need to *rescue* her."

They erupted into a semblance of laughter, the sound rusty, as if they hadn't laughed in a very long time. The grating sounds sent another round of shivers down her spine.

"Thank you, but I'm not in need of rescue." She turned and hurried in the opposite direction, on a path that would lead her directly back to Jacob. She wanted to run headlong into his strong embrace and never leave the warmth of his protective arms again. She wanted to tell him about the return of her vision. She wanted to say that she loved him. She suddenly realized that if a person waited too long, things could happen that would prevent those moments from ever happening. She prayed this wasn't one of them. She'd just regained her vision. She didn't want to lose her life.

A rough hand grasped her shoulder and spun her around. "It's rude to walk away from someone when they're talking."

"It's rude to place your hand upon a woman you've never met. Please release me at once," Hollan gritted out through her teeth.

"Ah, we've caught ourselves a spunky one, men."

They all laughed.

"You haven't *caught* me at all. I'm not a fish." Hollan fought off a wave of fear and held her ground.

"Ah, that's good! She's not a fish." The closest man mocked her.

Hollan tried to jerk from his grasp. "My husband will be along at any moment, and he won't be any too pleased to find you taking liberties with me."

If only it was true. She had no idea when Jacob would come looking for her, or even if he'd look at all.

"Then we'd best get back to the ship at once."

Her momentary relief turned into full-fledged panic when the closest man grabbed her roughly by the arm and dragged her toward their small wooden craft. She fought with everything she had, but that wasn't much. She might as well have been a feather for all the good it did.

She managed one more glance over her shoulder before they forced her into the boat, but the beach behind her remained empty.

⁊

Jacob finished his morning chores and headed down for breakfast. He stopped by his tiny room, which was in dire need of cleaning, and hurried to freshen it up. He didn't think Hollan would mind if he took a few minutes to tidy things. And if he didn't take the time to clean it now, he knew she'd eventually make her way out and clean it for him. He made the small bed—the only item pushed against the north wall of the room—and gathered a few pieces of clothes into a pile. He went outside to dump the pitcher of water that had sat forgotten upon his small table on the opposite side of the room before returning to put everything else back in place. Hooks on the remaining wall—the one opposite the door—held the only other clothes he owned.

When he decided the room was clean enough, he bundled up the clothes to be washed and headed over to greet his wife. He needed to talk to her about several things. He laid his laundry down near the washtub. Hollan would insist on doing his laundry, but he'd insist just as hard on doing it himself. Until they lived in the same house as husband and wife, he wouldn't expect her to do his clothes. And that very topic was one he intended to bring up. He'd been lonely last night and wanted things to change.

His feelings for Hollan hadn't ever wavered. Though their marriage hadn't come about quite the way they'd planned, they were still married. It was silly to live apart as they were. He just hoped she returned his feelings.

If she didn't, he'd be patient and wait. In time she'd surely grow to love him the same way he loved her.

Samson barked from inside the cottage, and Jacob grinned. The dog had heard his arrival. Surprisingly, he didn't hear Hollan hush him as usual with her melodic lilting voice. He'd come to rely on the familiar sound at the start of his day.

The early morning sun beat down on his head. Though the autumn nights were cooling down, the days were staying warm. Judging by the way the sun heated his back, today would be a hot one. The cool interior of the cottage beckoned him.

Jacob knocked and pushed open the door. "Good morning." Samson almost knocked him down in his hurry to get past and out into the yard, but Hollan didn't answer Jacob's greeting or bother to call Samson back.

With a whine, Samson wound himself around Jacob's legs.

"Hollan?" Jacob had a warning sensation that something wasn't right. He reached down and rubbed Samson on the head. "Where is she, boy?"

Samson glanced up at him with worried eyes.

Jacob moved into the empty room and let his eyes adjust to the dim interior. The table was set for one. The bed lay empty and neat. She'd taken time to pull the quilt up. She hadn't left in a hurry. The fire burned low, but she'd finished breakfast preparations before departing.

Maybe Fletcher had arrived early with the supply boat. Knowing Hollan, she'd have walked along with him to bring back supplies. Jacob glanced around. The few times he'd seen Fletcher, he hadn't wasted time. If he'd arrived at Hollan's door, he'd have carried something along. No sign of packages or supplies sat anywhere nearby.

He sighed. More than likely Hollan had left early in order to be alone. He tended to be a tad overbearing when it came to her. He knew she didn't like to be coddled, but he couldn't help himself. He hadn't protected her three years earlier when he'd needed to, and he didn't ever want to mess up again.

"Ah, I see." Jacob put his hands on his hips and looked at Samson. "She snuck out and left us both behind, is that it?" He walked to the table and surveyed the arrangement. "Well, we might as well show our appreciation as long as she went to the trouble of setting it all out."

The aroma of fresh-baked muffins permeated the room.

Samson wagged his tail. Jacob slipped into a chair and held a muffin high over his head. Samson stood on his hind legs, begged for a moment, then tired of the game and jumped to snatch the delicacy from Jacob's hand. He hurried away to eat his prize at his favorite place near the fire.

Jacob frowned and spread some butter on his own muffin. It was lonely here without Hollan. Without her presence, he'd have preferred to eat outside. But the flowers on the table showed the care she'd put into making the table pretty for him, and he wouldn't chance moving out front only to have her return and jump to the wrong conclusion.

As he ate, he mulled over his thoughts. He was sure Hollan was hiding something from him, and he was pretty sure he knew what her secret was. Ever since she'd recovered from her storm injuries, she'd been skittish. Something in her eyes had changed. She'd looked right into his eyes a few times before catching herself and turning away. He didn't want to jump to conclusions, either, but he was pretty sure she'd regained her vision, at least partially.

Why she wouldn't tell him, he didn't know. He'd tried to figure it out, but he'd stopped trying to understand her years ago. Whatever her reason, he'd find out soon enough.

He wanted to go after her but decided to give her a little more time. She'd been through some hard times. He wanted her to feel free and comfortable enough to confide in him whenever she decided the time was right. He wanted to move forward and have a life and a future with her. But a part of him worried that she might be having second thoughts. Maybe the return of her sight had her thinking she didn't need Jacob at all. If so, they needed to talk things out. She needed him, and he'd be the first to explain that fact to her.

Jacob wasn't one to tiptoe around a delicate circumstance— he preferred to plunge headfirst into every situation that crossed his path. He wouldn't do anything different with this one.

While he waited for her to return, he decided to tend the garden. A little hard work would clear his mind and help him think. The growing season was almost over, and only a few vegetables remained on the vines. He picked the tomatoes that were ready and put them in a nearby bucket. He pulled the last few weeds. Next year he'd like to expand the garden's size. If there would be a next year.

The thought led him back to wondering about Hollan.

He put down the hoe and walked over to the dunes. Hollan's small footprints led down toward the beach. The impressions of her bare feet showed that, once again, she'd left her boots behind.

Enough was enough. It was time for Jacob to go after his wife. He wanted to feel her in his arms.

He walked over to the cottage's open door. Samson lay sprawled just inside the cool interior.

"C'mon, boy. Want to go with me to find Hollan?"

Samson almost bowled him over in his hurry to get outside. Obviously he didn't intend to be left behind again. They headed up the path. Jacob stopped at the lighthouse door.

"I need to check on something first, boy. Stay."

Samson whined again but stayed where Jacob pointed. Jacob hurried up to the top of the lighthouse, no easy feat with the multiple stairs he had to climb. He stepped onto the platform that circled the top and looked out over the island. Samson lay where he left him down below.

He didn't see any sign of Hollan, but he did see a large ship offshore. An uneasy feeling settled over him. He walked a bit farther around the platform to a better vantage point. His breath caught as he located Hollan. A small boat had been pulled ashore.

His wife was so enraptured by whatever lay at her feet that she didn't appear to notice the men coming up from behind her. From the stealthy way they walked, he sensed they were up to no good.

"Hollan!" His voice blew away on the breeze. He spun

on his heel and rushed back to the stairs. He forced himself not to take them two at a time, a recipe for disaster. He couldn't afford to take a tumble. Hollan would be gone forever if that happened. She might be even as it was.

Samson stood at the ready, the hair on the nape of his neck standing on end.

"Go, boy, go to Hollan."

The dog tore away over the dunes and disappeared from sight. Jacob followed along as quickly as he could. The sand pulled at his heavy boots, slowing him even as he pushed to go faster. He didn't have a weapon, and he had no idea what he'd do once he reached her. But he'd do whatever was necessary to keep his wife safe.

God, please protect Hollan. Help me to reach her in time.

His feet slipped in the sand as he rounded the bend and approached the last place he'd seen his wife. He put his hand down to stop his tumble and landed on his knees. There was no sign of Hollan there now. The rowboat was halfway to the ship, too far away for him to have any hope of reaching it. From this distance, he couldn't tell if she was on board.

"Hollan!" No one aboard the small craft looked his way. The wind blew against him. They wouldn't hear him any more than Hollan had heard him from the lighthouse.

Samson stood chest deep at the water's edge and growled, confirming to Jacob what he already knew. Hollan was on the small boat.

nine

Hollan sat rigidly at the front of the small rowboat, glaring at her four captors. Two of them perched on the middle seat with their backs toward her while they rowed the small vessel closer to the large ship. The others sprawled on the remaining seat at the back of the boat, steadfastly glaring back at her. On closer observation she realized that one glared while the other tried his best to do the same through an obviously damaged eye. His left eye was swollen shut, and dark blue bruises spread outward from the edges.

She studied him, the smaller of the two, and winced. She vaguely remembered making the connection with her fist. "I'm truly sorry about your face."

An apology probably wouldn't make much difference at this time, but she figured she might as well try. She had no idea what awaited her aboard the ship, but surely arriving there after having assaulted one of the crew wouldn't work well in her favor.

The man didn't answer, but his good eye narrowed further.

"In my defense, you shouldn't sneak up behind a person like that. Surely you know the natural instinct is to swing around with a fist at the ready."

"I ne'er expected a lady to swing in such a way at all," the man muttered. He gingerly touched the area in question. "Or that a lady would connect with such accuracy."

"Because I'm a lady I'm supposed to just turn myself over to a bunch of scoundrels without a fight? Is that what you're saying?"

She folded her arms across her chest. Her bare foot tapped against the wooden floor with annoyance.

"It ain't polite to call people names, missy."

"It *isn't* polite to kidnap people, either." She raised one eyebrow and stared until he looked away.

The men in the middle rowed on without missing a beat. Each stroke brought them closer to their ship and farther away from Jacob. The methodical sound of their oars slapping against the water made Hollan want to scream. Every once in a while the wind would reverse and blow a whiff of their odor her way. She quickly figured out it was best to hold her breath under a direct assault and to breathe through her mouth the rest of the time.

Cloudless blue skies stretched high overhead. The sun shone down on the water, dappling on the tiny waves, just as it had when she was onshore. The gulls continued to scavenge for food. Nothing had changed, yet for her, nothing was the same.

While the injured man continued to look out over the water, the man beside him cleared his throat in an attempt to catch her attention. "Speakin' of faces, you're not sorry for mine?"

Hollan studied him for a moment and forced back the snide comment that first came to mind. She wasn't doing a very good job at keeping her thoughts kind. His perpetually bewildered expression wasn't likely any fault of his own. She noticed the bridge of his nose tilted at an odd angle, but she assumed it had been broken before. Then she noticed the trail of blood that led from his nose to his beard.

"Oh my." Her brows pulled close. "Did I do that to your nose, too?"

"You did."

"But when—?"

"You fought like a wildcat when we first grabbed you."

"Of course I did. Wouldn't you?"

"Then you snapped your head back into my nose."

"And I'm supposed to apologize to *you* for that? You grabbed me around the waist. Perhaps if you didn't snatch innocent women off beaches, you'd not end up injured."

"I told ya we should have left her there. She's gonna be nothin' but trouble." The man with the swollen eye returned his scowl to her.

"Couldn't leave her, Paxton. Cap'n gave us orders."

Hollan shook her head, trying to clear it. "He gave you orders to bring back a woman?"

"He gave us orders to bring back *you*." Swollen Eye—or Paxton—sneered.

"But how would he know about me?"

"Dunno. But he does, and you walked right into our arms."

"Hardly."

"Regardless, we didn't have any choice but to follow orders."

"You always have a choice," Hollan stated. "Are you nothing but slaves? This man—the captain—why would you allow him to order you around like that? Why would you want to do wrong on someone else's behalf?"

One of the men in the middle laughed. "It's his job to order us around." He glanced at the man beside him. "How dumb is this woman anyway?"

"I'm not dumb at all." Hollan tried to keep the hurt from her voice. "I'm only trying to understand why you'd choose to live this way."

Broken Nose gave her a sympathetic look. "There's no call to say mean things like that, Nate."

Hollan nodded. "Thank you. That was very kind."

He beamed at her. Nate sent her a glare.

"Look, if I had my way, you wouldn't be here at all. It's

bad luck for a woman to go aboard ship. Just look at what's happened to Paxton and Jonathon." Nate nodded toward the men.

So the man with the broken nose is apparently named Jonathon. "If you believe that, then return me to shore."

Nate didn't answer. He just kept rowing toward the vessel. They were almost to the ship. If she wanted out of this situation, she needed to act fast.

"Paxton. Jonathon. Please. You seem like nice enough men."

They both looked away.

"Idiotic is more like it," Nate snarled. "Now sit tight and be quiet. You're going to see the captain, like it or not."

Panic threatened to overwhelm Hollan, but she forced it away. She had to keep her thoughts straight. She sat quietly, not moving until they bumped against the side of the larger vessel.

"Ladies first." Nate laughed. He stood and grabbed her by the arm, pulling her to her feet.

Hollan looked back at him, blank. "I'm sure I don't know what you mean."

He motioned at the rope ladder that dangled over the side of the ship. "See that ladder in front of you? Climb it."

"I will not." She sat back down and folded her arms.

"Oh, but you will." He grabbed her arm again.

"You're hurting me."

"I'll hurt you a lot worse if you don't do as I say and get up that ladder."

Tears of anger and frustration poured down Hollan's cheeks. She snatched at the ropes and began her ascent. The skirt of her dress, still drenched from her trek when they dragged her through the water, snagged at her feet. She'd made it halfway up when she lost her grip. With a scream of terror, she plunged to the boat below. The boat rocked wildly back and forth but didn't capsize.

"Miss, are you all right?" Jonathon helped her to her feet.

"I—I think so. Nate broke my fall." She turned to thank him, but he lay still on the bottom of the boat. "Nate?"

The other man, the only one she hadn't injured at this point, stared at her, speechless.

"Nate was right. You *are* bad luck."

She rolled her eyes. "There's no such thing as bad luck."

The man leaned away from her, fear filling his face. "I don't know about you two"—he glanced over at Paxton and Jonathon—"but I'm not sticking around to see what she does next."

"Matt, what about Nate?"

"Leave 'im."

Matt turned and scaled the ladder and disappeared from sight in a way that left Hollan envious.

"I didn't mean to hurt him."

She took a step toward Jonathon. He looked from her to Paxton.

Paxton took advantage of her inattention and followed Matt up the ladder. "Don't let her get away, Jonathon."

"But—I—" Hollan had no idea where they thought she would go.

Paxton made it up the ladder with surprising grace and disappeared from sight.

"I guess it's just you and me, Jonathon." Hollan put on her most charming smile.

"You, me, and the dead man." Jonathon eased around Nate and headed for the ladder.

Hollan huffed out a breath. "He's not dead; I just knocked him unconscious—or something."

"No offense, ma'am. Deep down you seem like a nice lady and all. But I don't intend to stick around and see how you hurt the next man."

"I don't intend to hurt anyone!"

"All the same, you seem to have a knack."

Hollan knew if she let him go, she'd be free and she could escape. But the currents were rolling offshore as the tide went out, and she knew she'd never have the strength on her own to get back safely. She'd be washed out to sea, which at the moment actually sounded appealing compared to the thought of whatever unknown situation awaited her aboard ship.

Before she could think things through, she was suggesting an idea to Jonathon. "If you help me get back to shore, I'll help you start a new life. You don't have to do this."

He stopped. "I'd never make it off your island alive."

"Yes, you would. My husband and I would protect you."

Jonathon hesitated.

"Please."

His bewildered face glanced from her to the ship's rail and back.

"What's going on down there?" a voice called from above. The muzzle of a rifle edged into sight from over the rail.

Hollan glanced at Jonathon. "The captain?"

Jonathon nodded.

"Get the prisoner up here at once!" the voice bellowed.

"We have to go. I'm sorry." Jonathon took her arm, his touch gentle.

Hollan felt the panic welling. "We still have time. We can push off and go ashore. My husband will be waiting."

"He's a very good shot, ma'am. I'm truly sorry. We hafta do as he says."

Hollan let silent tears fall in resignation as she put decorum aside and climbed the ladder to the top.

❧

A strong set of arms reached over the edge and pulled Hollan the last few feet up and over the top of the rail.

Hollan swung around and landed awkwardly on her hands and knees. "Thanks. I think."

"Welcome aboard the *Lucky Lady*."

"Funny choice of name for a boat since your entire crew begs to differ."

"Speaking of crew, it sounds like you might have an idea about what made them scatter."

The masculine voice sounded strangely familiar.

She ignored the offered hand and remained on her knees. She slowly raised her gaze. "David?"

"Indeed. Are you happy to see me?"

"I'm not sure." Would Jacob's brother show her favor? Had he changed his ways? Would he see to her safety, or would he continue his mutiny? She answered her own questions. He'd sent for her. And he certainly hadn't done so in order to congratulate her on her recent nuptials.

His laughter chilled her to the bone.

"Paxton!"

Paxton rounded a corner but kept his distance.

"Gather the rest of the men."

David didn't offer her further assistance. Hollan was content to remain on her knees—the more distance she could have between him and the rail, the better.

A few moments later her kidnappers reappeared.

David glanced at them and then looked again. "What happened to you?"

"*She* happened to us." Paxton pointed.

David stalked along the deck. "You're telling me this wisp of a woman gave one of you a black eye and the other a broken nose?"

"She did. And she kilt Nate." Jonathon sent her an apologetic look. "But I don't think she meant to do it."

"She killed—" David's eyes widened as he hurried to the side and peered down at the smaller craft where Nate still lay sprawled on the bottom of the boat. "But how?"

Hollan sighed. "I didn't kill him. He's merely unconscious." Her brows furrowed. "Or at least I think that's all it is."

"Well, don't just leave him down there. Someone bring him up."

"How we gonna do that, Cap'n?"

"Think of something."

Jonathon's studious expression made him look as if he was in pain. "We can wrap a rope around his neck and haul him up that way."

Hollan's eyes widened in horror.

Paxton rolled his own eyes. "That'd be called a noose, Jonathon. Wanna finish Nate off completely?"

"We'll tie it under his arms, then."

"That should work." Paxton glanced at Matt. "You climb down to the boat and tie the rope around him. Jonathon and I will pull him up."

David shook his head. "Or you *could* just raise the rowboat into place and then lift him over the side."

"Good idea, Cap'n. Makes more sense." Jonathon grimaced. "We can do that easy. We'll get right on it."

"See that you do." David stalked away toward the main deck, shaking his head. "And one of you take Hollan down below. Secure her in the hold."

"You go with her, Jonathon." Matt motioned her way. "Paxton and I will take care of Nate."

"Afraid to be alone with me, are you?" Hollan knew better than to goad Matt, but she couldn't resist. If the level of fear in his eyes when he looked at Hollan was any indication, the man still felt she had the ability to cause them all harm with nothing more than her presence.

"I'm not afraid of you, miss." Jonathon led the way. Hollan's moment of levity passed when she realized they were going below deck. The chances of escape were few, but if she remained below deck they'd be nonexistent.

"God is sufficient for all our needs, Hollan."

Hollan remembered Jacob's words from just before the hurricane. He'd been right then, and she felt sure God would bring her through this, too. A momentary sense of peace swept through her. Though this was a different kind of storm, the words couldn't be any truer.

Jonathon led the way, and Hollan stayed close at his heels. The ship's gloomy interior depressed her. It took a few minutes for her eyes to adjust. She could see the dim shapes of several other prisoners. Jonathon led her to a nearby pole and waited expectantly. Hollan stared back, not sure what it was he wanted her to do.

"You need to wrap your arms around the pole." Jonathon waved a piece of rope he'd snagged from a nearby hook. "I have to tie you up."

"Tie me—?" Hollan sputtered. Suddenly she realized the gravity of her situation. If she was tied up below deck and they set sail, Jacob would never find her. A sob forced its way through her terror. "But Jonathon—"

"I'm sorry, miss. I have to follow orders. I'll be back to check on you soon."

"Don't leave me in the dark. I've had nothing but darkness for so long. You don't understand."

"I really am sorry." He tied her hands around the pole and left to go above deck.

"Oh, God, what am I to do?" Hollan whispered the words aloud. None of the emaciated men around her moved. She couldn't tell if they were dead or alive. Surely she hadn't been left alone in a room full of dead people. She shuddered. Based on the odors sifting around her, she wouldn't be surprised. Where was that sense of peace? It was as if she'd left it above deck before she descended. She felt as if she'd entered her own personal version of hell.

I will never forsake you. A gentle breeze caressed her hot skin. She looked around but saw nothing amiss. *God is here with me!* Hollan knew the fact as well as she knew her own name. She wasn't alone.

God had a plan for her. She didn't know what it was, but she rested in the knowledge that He'd led her here for a purpose.

"Hollan."

Had God spoken her name aloud?

She glanced around and saw movement to her right.

"Hollan." The raspy voice came again, stronger this time.

It couldn't be. Her mind must be playing tricks on her. But she hadn't imagined that voice.

"Papa?" Her voice broke. *Please, God, let it be so!*

"It's me, daughter."

Hollan pulled at her ties, but they only tightened.

"Papa!"

"Don't fight the ropes, Hollan. You'll only cause yourself pain."

"But, Papa, what are you doing here?"

"Same thing as you, apparently." His soft laugh flowed through her like a salve. "I've missed you so much. I know you had to worry."

"I knew you were alive." Hollan smiled into the darkness. God had indeed had a plan. He'd sent her to rescue her father.

ten

Jacob couldn't believe the mess his wife had gotten herself into this time. How could she not have seen the crew's arrival? He cringed as he thought through the words. Maybe her vision hadn't returned after all. And here he'd been thinking she was keeping something from him. He felt awful. He'd just found her again, and he wouldn't lose her now. He had to get her back.

The ship was too far out for him to swim to her, and though the tide was going out, he knew they'd never make it back to shore, even if he had their missing boat. The boat wouldn't have helped anyway. They kept it on the inland side of the island. He couldn't go after her. He'd never make it through the currents. He paced back and forth on the shore, trying to come up with a plan. Without his own boat, he had no choice but to watch as she floated away with the crew. He hadn't felt this helpless since the night his father and brothers had ransacked the town.

Samson remained at the water's edge, staring out over the ocean. Every once in a while he'd look at Jacob like, *Why aren't you* doing *something?*

Jacob returned to the dog's side and watched until the rowboat was too far away to see very well. Even if Hollan looked around, she wouldn't see him now.

He turned back and headed at a fast pace toward the lighthouse. Samson trotted alongside him. "We'll get her back, boy, don't worry."

Jacob sounded a lot more confident than he felt. He took

the steps of the lighthouse two at a time. Maybe he couldn't go after her, but what he could do was keep watch, take notice of anything he could about the ship, and track their progress. When Fletcher came their way with the supply boat, Jacob would summon help.

The crew of the ship didn't appear to be in any hurry. They lingered offshore even as the sun set. The full moon tracked their progress as they curved around the end of the island and sailed toward the mouth of the river.

Jacob's heart skipped a beat. If the captain continued his present course, they'd soon be near the far side of the island. The channel narrowed on that side in a way that if Jacob left now, he might be able to get on board the ship.

࿐

The thud of heavy feet lumbering down the stairs pulled Hollan from a restless sleep. She found herself curled up on the filthy floor.

"Jacob." Her voice was hoarse as she whispered his name. Perhaps he'd found a way to come for her. She peered through the darkness but knew immediately that Jacob would never arrive in such a noisy fashion. Her heart sank. He'd come in quietly, not wanting to rouse suspicion, and would sneak her—and her father—away without anyone the wiser. Whoever descended the stairs now had no concerns about drawing attention. Quite the contrary, from the noise the person made on the stairs, he wanted to alert everyone to his presence.

Her legs were numb from hours spent in an awkward position. Earlier, during the night when she couldn't bear the thought of sitting or lying on the slimy wood floor, she'd placed her forehead against the pole and settled into a squat. She hadn't slept well at all. The tormented moans of the other prisoners had her on edge. Throughout the night the sound of tiny claws skittering across the floor made her shudder. She could well imagine what type of creature the scurrying feet belonged to. And the cloying heat and putrid odors permeated every breath she took.

Each time she'd doze off, she'd fall forward, and the motion would jerk her back awake. Exhaustion had her on edge. She didn't even want to imagine what David had planned for her. And she hoped she'd never find out. He wouldn't have anything in store for her if she could help it. She only had to figure out an escape plan before the madman sent for her.

"Cap'n wants to see you on deck."

The escape plan would have to wait.

Paxton stood beside her. When she couldn't rise on her own, he grabbed her arm and pulled her roughly to her feet. Her legs tingled.

"You seem to take great pleasure in yanking me around by my arm." His bad eye made him look demented in the dimness.

"A lot of things bring me great pleasure. Dealing with you does not."

"Leave her alone!"

Papa.

Her father's voice brought her a measure of peace, even though he couldn't do anything to help her at the moment. She had to focus on a plan that would get them both away from here. In the meantime, it wouldn't hurt to pray.

Lord, I'm not sure what is in store for me while You have me on this ship, but I pray that You'll protect us. Please help Jacob to know where we are, and keep my father safe.

She turned her attention to Paxton. "What does David want with me?"

Paxton shrugged as he untied the knots in the rope that held her hands prisoner. Once he released her, she almost fell on her face.

"You'll get your sea legs in due time."

"I don't intend to be around long enough for that to happen."

Paxton laughed. "I don't see that you have a choice."

"I'll find a way out of here."

"You will, huh? We'll see about that."

He half-dragged her to the stairs. They exited the stairwell onto the main deck, and the bright early morning light shot a dagger of pain through Hollan's head. She closed her eyes briefly, let them adjust, and then squinted through them. Her vision remained clear. She eased her eyes open after a moment and located David at the ship's helm.

She left Paxton's grasp and plowed forward. "David."

"Ah, good morning, Hollan. I trust you slept well?"

She ignored his ridiculous question and instead asked one of her own, echoing her earlier one to Paxton. "What do you want with me?"

"It seems I need to go up the inland channel. In order to do so, I'll happen to need a guide."

Hollan couldn't hold back her smirk. He needed a guide, and he'd chosen the least able person to comply. "You do realize I lost my eyesight three years ago?"

He glanced at her, his forehead wrinkled. "You can't see at all? If that were true, you wouldn't have found your way so easily to me just now."

"Whether I can or can't see right now doesn't matter. What does matter is that I haven't seen this pass or much of anything else since. You've chosen and kidnapped the wrong person to help you."

"You can stop looking so amused." David's scowl deepened. "I'm sure the pass hasn't changed all that much over the past three years."

"Do you seriously believe that?" Hollan's jaw dropped. "Do

you not remember the storms we get around here? Nothing ever remains the same."

Not in the least. The storms damaged everything. Her experiences attested to that.

"Then you'd better pray the storms haven't changed the pass."

Hollan started to refuse. She wouldn't guide him anywhere.

"If you don't abide by my terms, your father will pay the price for your rebellion."

That quieted her. She wouldn't do anything to bring more pain to her father.

An idea began to formulate in her mind. When they rounded the end of the island to enter the pass, Jacob would be at the closest point to help them. At least he would be if he knew she was aboard the ship and he'd been tracking their progress.

She couldn't stand the thought of the alternative. If he hadn't figured out where she'd disappeared to, why would he care about one more ship offshore? She hadn't a clue where her father had gone when he'd disappeared. Why would Jacob have any idea about where she'd gone? Even if he went to look for her, she'd have disappeared just as completely as her father.

She decided that just in case Jacob hadn't figured out her whereabouts, her plan had to be something she could fulfill on her own. The pass was treacherous in the best of times. Maybe she could use that to her advantage.

"The currents are very strong at the mouth of the river."

"Thank you. We'll prepare for rougher waters. In the meantime, you'll remain below deck. I'll send for you when I'm ready."

Hollan thought hard. If she stayed above deck, she might have a chance to catch Jacob's attention. But if she went below, perhaps her father could help with suggestions to guide them through the channel. She didn't want to return to the stench of the dark, dank hold, but if she needed to, she'd make use of the option.

In the meantime, she'd try to stay above deck. "I'd prefer to remain up here if you don't mind."

"I don't recall giving you a choice."

"I'll stay out of the way." Hollan started for the rear of the ship. Maybe she'd spot Jacob and would at least be encouraged that he was looking for her. "I'll just settle in up there where I can observe the channel and the conditions."

A rough hand grabbed her arm. David leaned close. "You'll do as I say and go below."

His menacing blue eyes peered into hers. Hollan fought back a chill. The man's eyes were empty. He had no trace of heart or soul. The hold suddenly sounded inviting in light of this realization.

"Fine." She pulled her arm loose.

He pushed her forward toward Paxton. "Stow her below until we're ready."

The dirty hem of her dress tripped her as Paxton led the way downstairs.

Her father waited anxiously where she'd left him.

"Hollan. Are you well?"

"I'm fine, Papa."

He didn't speak again until Paxton had tied her wrists around the pole. As the man shuffled upstairs, her father leaned forward. "What did he want with you?"

"He wants me to guide him through the channel."

A soft chuckle carried over to her. "Did you explain?"

"I did. But, Papa—" She leaned nearer, wishing she could see him better in the darkness. "I can see clearly again. During the past couple of months, my vision would come and go, but now it stays."

"That's wonderful!"

"It is, but I'm not sure it'll help me guide the ship through the pass." She heard him change position. "Are *you* well, Father?"

"I'm fine." He shifted again. "Nothing the light of day won't fix, along with getting back to our island. I sorely miss your cooking."

Hollan laughed. "That says a lot, Papa. My cooking hasn't ever been all that great."

"I miss it all the same."

"Papa, what's going on? Why are you here?"

"David thought he could take me from my position as lightkeeper and use it to his advantage if he's captured. He wanted me to lead him through the inland waterway, but I refused." He let out a breath. "I refused to help the scoundrel. I had no idea he'd go after you next."

Her eyes had adjusted to the dim interior, but it was still pretty dark. "What are we going to do?"

"You're going to do exactly what they tell you. I don't want them angry with you. I don't want David to get violent. If he hurts you, you could lose your vision again—or worse. I won't have you risk that. Just do as he says, and let me figure something out."

Another figure stole quietly down the stairs. His furtive movements drew Hollan's attention. "Who is that, Papa?"

"I'm not sure. Keep quiet. Don't draw attention. I don't trust any of the crew around you."

Hollan settled low and huddled near the pole. The bulky figure carried a mop and moved through the men, stopping now and then to peer closely at each person as he passed. Hollan's heart beat quicker and sweat rolled down her face as the figure turned their way.

"Stay low, Hollan. Duck your head."

She did as her father instructed. The shadowy form loomed over her. He leaned close. Hollan kept her head down, praying she'd be left alone. The figure squatted down and leaned in close to her ear.

"Get away from her." Hollan's father's voice held a hint of panic.

Hollan knew it would kill him to watch if she was attacked and he couldn't do anything about it. She reacted instinctively, kicking the aggressor with her foot. A soft laugh rewarded her attempt.

"My darling wife. A bare foot does nothing to me. Though based on the stench of this hold, I might catch a nasty illness by connecting with your foot."

"Jacob?" A sob caught on Hollan's throat. "Is it really you?"

"It's me."

He wrapped his arms around her and held her close for a moment. She leaned nearer and drew in his scent. "You smell wonderful."

That comment drew a laugh out of him. "You seem to be in good humor. Are you all right?"

"I'm fine now that you're here." She savored the feel of his strong arms around her. She'd never take his presence or touch or encouragement for granted again.

"Want to tell me what you're doing here?"

"Rescuing him." She gestured toward her father in the dim light.

"Rescuing someone with your arms tied tightly around a pole. And whom would you be rescuing?"

"My father. He's alive, just as I said. What are *you* doing here?"

"Rescuing my wife and apparently helping her rescue her father."

Hollan laughed quietly. "I just about had my plan figured out."

Jacob trailed her arms to where they were tied around the post. "So I see. And your capture by the crew, that was all part of your plan?"

"Not exactly, but once it happened and I knew my father was here, I knew God brought me here for that purpose. I just needed to figure out what the plan was."

"Well, I'm here now to help." Jacob put a finger against her lips. "Be quiet now; we don't want to draw any more attention our way. I'm going to be close, but I'll continue to pose as one of the crew until I get *my* plan figured out."

"Papa's right beside me, one pole over. He's a little worse for wear, but he says he's fine."

Jacob caressed Hollan's hair with a gentle hand before moving to her father's side. "Gunter? I'm so happy to see you're alive, sir."

Hollan grinned as she watched her two favorite men interact.

"I'm happy to see you, too. My daughter told me about your marriage and all that you've done for her. I appreciate that you took it upon yourself to watch out for her. It's not an easy task."

"Papa!"

"Well, it's true. Now, Jacob, tell me what you've come up with to get us out of here."

"I haven't figured out the details on that myself. I saw the crew take Hollan, but I was too far away to do anything about it. I watched the ship from the lighthouse until I saw the present course. I was concentrating on getting aboard but didn't get far enough to figure out a rescue in the event I was successful. I've spent most of my time searching for your daughter aboard ship."

"Well, son, you're aboard now and you've found my daughter, so you'd best get to figuring out our escape."

"Have you made friends with any of the other prisoners?"

"No. None of them have tried to communicate with me. I'm not even sure some of them are alive. From what I can tell, they're all worse off than I am. I think some of them are former crew members from whenever the present crew took over the ship."

"I see." Jacob moved back to Hollan's side and took her hand. "I'm going back up to have a look around. I'll return soon."

"Don't leave us."

Her father leaned forward. "They're coming for Hollan soon. They want her to lead them through the channel."

Jacob hesitated. "That might work."

"What might work?" Hollan didn't like his tone of voice.

"Hollan, if you're on deck, you'll be that much closer to escape."

"And if my eyesight falters?"

"We'll worry about that if and when it does."

"I won't leave without you and my father."

"We'll all go together. But I need you free and above deck." He turned to her father. "Do they check your ties often?"

"Never."

"Good. That'll work in our favor, too. I'm going to untie you. I don't want you to move until we're ready to go. Hollan, you'll have to get the ship stuck in a shallow, narrow part of the channel. Try to guide them close to the island. While they're unloading supplies in order to lighten the load, we'll make our move. I'll come down here to get your father. You get off ship and head for the cabin on the island."

"I won't leave without my father. I already told you that."

Papa motioned to her. "Hollan, you'll do as your husband says."

"But—"

"But nothing." Jacob's voice was calm but commanding. "If you're out of the way and safe, I can better help your father."

Hollan bit back her next words. They'd discuss this later. She watched as Jacob untied her father's hands.

"Try to stand. I want to see if you can walk."

Her father stood, but he wavered. Hollan wanted to cry. Her normally strong father was thin and very weak.

"I'll be fine. You go do what you need to do. I'll work on my stamina while you're gone."

"Hollan, I'll leave you tied up until the captain sends for you."

"Jacob." Hollan knew the next words wouldn't be easy for Jacob to hear.

Jacob paused.

"The captain—he's your brother. David."

"*David's* behind this?" Jacob spat. "Why am I not surprised?"

"Promise me you won't rush into anything."

"I won't worry about David until I have both you and your father safely ashore."

Hollan didn't like the innuendo behind his words. She had a feeling that as soon as Jacob had them safe, he'd risk his own life by going after his brother.

eleven

Hollan didn't have to wait long before David summoned her. Paxton's heavy boots stomped down the stairs, echoing through the dim interior like a death sentence. She sent a frantic look at her father as the other man slopped through the muck and headed their way.

"It's going to be fine, Hollan. Jacob's watching out for you. God's on our side. Say your prayers and do what David says. Don't do anything dangerous. Let Jacob make the decisions that need to be made. Watch for him and be alert for any sign he sends you. He won't let anything happen to you."

"But if things don't go as we plan. . ."

"Our plans aren't what matter," her father interrupted her. "Do what you need to do, daughter. But above all else, keep your temper under control. Think before you act."

He lowered his voice as Paxton drew near. "Keep in mind what will happen to Jacob if you act in a rash manner. If he thinks you'll be hurt, he'll intervene before he's ready. The two of you are fully outnumbered by the crew. The timing for our escape needs to be perfect. If at all possible, do only what Jacob told you to do. Find a way to get the ship stuck on a sandbar and let him handle things from there. Remember what I've taught you about the currents. If you see your opportunity to get off the ship, take it and make your escape. Jacob and I will soon follow."

"But if you don't. . ."

"We will."

"*If* you don't. . . ?"

"Find a place to hide and watch for Fletcher to come."

"He's due back tomorrow."

"Then you'll go to him."

Paxton tripped over a body sprawled at his feet. He kicked at the immobile form.

Hollan glared at him as he continued his trek their way. The man was deplorable.

"Your emotions are written all over your face, Hollan, even in this dark place. Keep your thoughts hidden. If David thinks you're anything but compliant. . .it won't go well." Her father's quiet plea drifted her way. His gaunt face looked tortured for a moment. "Do this for your mother. David caused her to do what she did. I'll explain everything later. But we need to make things right. Do your part to get us safely off ship, and we'll talk when we meet back up."

Frustration edged through Hollan. She didn't know what the next few hours would bring, but she prayed they'd bring closure for all three of them.

"C'mon. Cap'n says it's time."

"Time for. . . ?" Hollan stalled.

"Let's go." Paxton ignored her comment and untied her. He reached for her arm.

Hollan scurried to her feet and backed away from him with her arms raised in defense. She knew her father would go after Paxton if he made any untoward moves. She couldn't let her father expose the fact that his hands were no longer tied.

"I'm ready. I don't need your assistance." The boat lurched, and Hollan pitched forward, plowing into him with her head.

Paxton let out his breath with a *whoosh*.

"Sorry. I didn't mean to." Hollan sent her father a quick glance and shrug. He remained in place, though his features were pained. "I lost my balance when the ship shifted."

"So I noticed," Paxton snapped. "See that you don't do it again."

"I'll do my best," Hollan snapped back.

She hadn't intended to get that close to the smelly man in the first place. As it was, she felt in dire need of a sweet-smelling bath. If she ever got out of here, she'd soak in an herb-filled bath for a full day. The hold's odors had permeated her nose and surely everything she wore. How her father had tolerated it for as long as he had she didn't know. It had to pain him to remain below deck, a free man, and not be able to do anything about it.

They exited the stairwell, and Hollan gasped for her first breath of fresh air topside. A gentle breeze blew her way, and even the fishy scent that rode along with it smelled pure after breathing in the stale air down below for the short time she'd been back down there. Now that the sun had risen higher in the sky, the day was clear and sunny. Inspiration bubbled up from deep inside. They had to make this work. Hollan wanted off the ship.

A movement to her left caught her attention. *Jacob.* He peeked up at her from beneath the rim of his hat. The bedraggled outfit he wore made him blend in perfectly with the crew. She twisted the corner of her mouth up in acknowledgment before diverting her gaze.

"What do you find so amusing?" Paxton glared around at the crew.

"There's nothing amusing about my situation. I'm simply rejoicing in the fact that I'm out of that pit for a time. Surely you can understand that."

Paxton scowled at her. "Don't try anything stupid. The captain doesn't tolerate anything close to what he considers mutiny."

Hollan didn't answer. She busied herself looking for Jonathon. Next to Jacob, he seemed her only ally. And though she wasn't sure his kindness would be enough to allow him to stand up against David and his crew, she had a feeling the man had a soft spot somewhere deep inside. If need be, she'd use that to both of their advantage.

"Are you ready?" David didn't waste time with pleasantries.

Hollan walked up beside him, shading her eyes with her hand as she scoured the water ahead of them. *How to best get the* Lucky Lady *stuck?* According to her father, it wouldn't be hard.

"We need to stay with the darker water. The path is narrow. Are you sure you don't want to turn around and go by sea?"

"What I want is for you to do as I ask. Don't question my decisions." He shifted his stance. "I have authorities looking for me on the open waters. I want to use this waterway to avoid a—shall we say—unpleasant outcome."

"You mean you want to avoid your imminent arrest." Hollan smiled up at him.

"I will not be arrested." His face turned purple. "I won't be captured alive."

She frowned. "Which means you'd prefer to be captured dead? But how will that benefit you or your crew? I'm not sure I understand."

"Must you always be talking?" He sighed with exasperation. "I don't intend to be captured at all. Now focus on the task before you."

Hollan laughed. "You sound like my father. That's his favorite thing to say."

David stared at her. "My crew doesn't dare to speak to me the way you do."

"Your crew? Is that what you call them? Better it be said that they are your slaves." She muttered the last part in a quieter voice, but he apparently heard her.

"Every man here has a right to leave anytime he chooses."

"Maybe—but only with a knife in his back or a bullet through his head."

David sputtered. "What gives you the right to speak to me like that? Your father has spoiled you. I'm not sure what my brother ever saw in a quick-tongued woman like you."

"Jacob saw my heart."

"And then, apparently, you drove him away."

"I didn't drive him away." His comment cut to her very soul. Jacob hadn't left her because of anything she'd done to him— had he? She shouldn't listen to this man. Her father told her to focus on the tasks set before her, and here she goaded the evil man instead of focusing on her responsibilities. She couldn't help spitting out one more remark. "That isn't true."

"Aw, have I hit a nerve?"

Hollan stared at the water ahead. "No, but you're about to hit that sandbar." She pointed a finger straight out in front of them.

David swore and spun the wheel hard to the left. Hollan hid her impertinent smile. A cough slightly behind and to her left drew her attention. Jacob worked nearby, and she was sure he'd overheard their discussion.

"You did that on purpose," David snapped.

"I did. I pointed out the obvious. But next time you'd rather I allow you to hit the object we're heading for?"

"No!" He reached up to adjust his hat then glared her way. "You're trying to distract me so we'll run aground."

"I'm hardly *trying* to distract you. Do you think I enjoy your attention?" Hollan huffed out a breath of exasperation. "And if my intent was to distract you so that you'd run the ship aground, *why* would I warn you when I saw the sandbar coming?"

"I guess you have a point."

She pushed her hair out of her face and gave a distracted wave toward their left. "You'll want to steer hard to the left for a bit. The current here runs strong and pushes to the right." Strong enough to embed them securely just off the island's shore if things worked out as she planned. Hollan set her mouth in a pout and crossed her arms in front of her.

"You don't have to sound so offended."

"And why shouldn't I after I save the ship from going aground only to have you berate me?"

The ship missed the sandbar and gently drifted to the left. David relaxed his hold, and the wheel spun out of his grip. They picked up speed as the current forced them into the smaller channel. "Wha—?"

He frantically fought the wheel. "I thought you said the current pushes to the right!" His voice rose in pitch and shook with anger. His eyes held a hint of panic.

They headed toward the island at a fast pace. Hollan sidled over to grab hold of the ship's rail. "Did I say the current pushes to the right? I meant you'd need to steer right because the current pushes to the left. Sorry." She raised her voice to be heard. "You can correct the ship's course, right?"

"You did this on purpose!" David screeched. "All hands on deck—*now!*"

Strong hands grabbed Hollan from behind and dragged her away from the captain. "Get down!"

Jacob's voice.

Hollan did as he said. She hadn't quite hunkered all the way down when the ship went hard aground. Barrels and crew went tumbling across deck. David flew to the right, cracked his head on the rail, and landed facedown, motionless.

"I need to go to him. I did this." Hollan's breath caught in her throat. Had her actions killed the man? She hadn't planned for anyone to get hurt. The ship listed heavily toward the mainland. "I didn't intend to hurt him."

"Well, he does intend to hurt you. Remember that. You're going nowhere but off this ship. As soon as you're clear, head for the cabin immediately." Jacob lifted her to her feet, and they took off across the deck at a run. He dodged both crew and debris as they went. No one looked their way with all the chaos. "David isn't worth your concern. Not right now."

"But my father."

"I'm sure your father is already on his way up here. I'll return to help him as soon as I get you safely on your way."

They reached the ladder. No one bothered with them as the crew frantically threw barrels and supplies off ship in an effort to stop her pitching.

Hollan peered cautiously over the side. "It's a long way down. Coming up was bad enough. My dress! The skirt will. . ."

Jacob snatched a knife from the sheath he wore around his waist and spun her around. He grabbed her skirt and hacked it off at the knees.

"Jacob!" Hollan sputtered.

"It's filthy and ruined. You'll move faster this way. Your skirt won't pull you under the water."

He resheathed the knife and eased her over the edge. "Hold the ladder tight. If you lose your grip, push off so you don't bump against the ship. Get away as quickly as possible in case she shifts. You don't want to be crushed beneath her."

"And there is a very pleasant thought with which to bid me good-bye."

"And a very likely scenario if you don't get out of the way." He hesitated and grasped her upper arms. "I love you, Hollan." He pulled her close for a quick peck on her lips. "Now go. Get out of sight. Move quickly."

She ducked below the ship's rail and headed carefully

down the ladder. Her hands shook, and she prayed she'd not lose her grip. The ship's rounded sides made the endeavor awkward and hindered her descent. Her foot slipped, and she flailed for a moment before finding purchase again.

Just as she regained her footing, something large catapulted past her. She ducked with a scream. Another piece of her dress tore off as the large object shot past, but she was able to keep hold of the ladder.

Hollan lowered her foot again and felt for the next rope step. Something else fell from above, and again it barely missed her. A sob tore loose. Were they throwing things at her? Had they figured out the plan? Had someone noticed her missing?

She pushed herself to move faster but again lost her footing. This time her fingers slipped from their hold, too, and she plunged to the water below. The momentum sent her into a downward spiral under the water even as she fought to return to the surface. After a few panicked moments, her toes finally hit sand, and she pushed hard against the bottom. She broke through the surface of the water and gasped in a huge lungful of air.

A barrel splashed down beside her, barely missing her head. She swam in place and looked around for a safer location to wait out the barrage of debris. Only one area would offer her protection. She swam to the boat and hunkered down out of sight, slightly under the rounded side. If the ship shifted at all, she'd be crushed beneath it, just as Jacob had warned.

≈

Jacob hurried across the tilting deck and prepared to go below just as Gunter surfaced. A small man with a crooked nose assisted him. Jacob raised an eyebrow in question.

"It's all right. Jonathon here offered me his assistance. He said he failed Hollan when she needed him, and he wanted to make things right with me." Gunter looked around. "Where is she?"

"I've already helped her over the edge. She should be well on her way to the shore." Another glance at Gunter's helper reassured Jacob that the man didn't have any ulterior motives. The man nervously watched the actions of the crew but didn't try to draw attention. David still lay where they'd left him. "We need to get out of here before he comes around. He isn't going to be in a very good mood."

"Does the man *have* a good mood?" Gunter muttered.

"Not that I've ever seen, but we don't want to be here to see what he does when his perpetually bad mood gets worse."

They helped Gunter to the side of the ship where Jacob had last seen Hollan. He peered over and saw no sign of her. Hopefully that meant she'd made it to safety. Two members of the crew appeared, carrying a large barrel between them. They staggered up beside Jacob.

"Can you give us a hand in gettin' this over? It's mighty heavy," one of the men gasped.

"Set it down." Panic coursed through Jacob. "Have you thrown other things over this side?"

"Yep. We needed to lighten the load."

Jacob leaned over and again searched the water for any sign of Hollan. If a barrel had hit her. . .

He saw a piece of fabric from her dress floating on the water, but he didn't see any other physical signs of her. Surely if she'd been hit she'd still be in sight. He breathed easier and looked at the men. "Not on this side, you don't."

The man surveyed him suspiciously. "Why not?"

Jonathon stepped up beside him. "Ya see how the ship lists? Ya might knock a hole in the side."

"Oh. I hadn't thought about that."

"Head on over there with the barrel"—Jacob pointed to

the far side—"and I'll be right behind you to help."

The two men struggled to lift the large container.

Jacob rolled his eyes. "Can I offer a suggestion?"

One looked at the other. "I guess."

"Roll the barrel to the other side. Don't carry it."

"That might work." The deckhand looked skeptical. "We can try."

They laid it on its side and pushed.

"No, you'll want to—" Jacob shook his head as the barrel picked up pace on its journey across the deck. It took out two men before slamming into the wooden rail on the far side. "Never mind."

The men took off at a run, and Jacob quickly turned around. "Come on, we need to get out of here before someone else comes along."

Jonathon helped lift Gunter over the side. Jacob looked at Jonathon. "Are you coming with us?"

"No. I'm needed here. You go. I'll keep watch as I work, and I'll offer a diversion if need be."

"We appreciate it, Jonathon."

"Tell Hollan I'm sorry. I couldn't help her before, but I hope she's safe now."

"Thank you."

Jacob glanced around, then slipped over the rail and followed Gunter down the ladder. He heard a soft *splash* below as Gunter entered the water. Jacob made quick work of dropping down beside him.

"Let's go. We need to get away from the ship."

"Jacob!"

Jacob glanced around and saw Hollan clinging to the large vessel's side.

"Woman! Don't you ever listen?"

"I *do* listen, but before I could get away, huge objects

started raining down on me from above."

"I think we've stayed the falling objects. Let's get out of here."

They only had a short swim before their feet touched bottom. Jacob reached back and assisted Hollan until her feet reached solid ground.

"I'm fine, I'm fine. Go, go, go!" Hollan's panicked voice urged him on. She stepped up beside him and helped assist her father.

She started toward the shelter of the trees.

"Not that way. We need to stay in the water."

"They'll see us."

"Jonathon is helping from the ship. He won't let anyone approach this side. It's tilting away from us. The crew is busy on the other side, trying to lighten the load so the ship will rise off the sandbar."

"Why not go into the cover of the trees?"

"The foliage is too dense. We have to get to the path, but we need to stay in the water so they can't follow our tracks."

They reached a shallow creek and turned to follow it into the trees.

"We're safe for now, Hollan. Their guns won't reach this far. No one can see us."

Hollan's legs gave out. Jacob caught her and held her close.

"We're safe," he murmured again. "It's going to be okay."

"I need a quick rest." Gunter climbed out of the creek and sank to the ground nearby. He leaned against a tree. "What's the plan from here?"

"We'll go to Amos's cabin."

Hollan pulled her face away from Jacob's chest and looked up at him. Her eyes were smudged with exhaustion, but she stared directly at him. He watched her eyes soften as she surveyed his features. Her mouth broadened into a smile.

"You're a sight for sore eyes."

"Your vision seemed to be intact the entire time we were on the ship. Is it fully restored?"

"At first it came back in bits and pieces, but yes, I can consistently see clearly now. And thank you."

"Why are you thanking me?"

"You came after me. You rescued us."

"You're my wife. I'll always come for you." He kissed the tip of her nose. "But about the return of your vision. . ."

She smirked and turned his words on him. "We'll discuss it later."

Gunter motioned for their attention. "If you two can try to concentrate, we do have some pretty angry men aboard that ship who would probably like to recapture us. I'd like to get some more space between them and us. I think I can walk some more now."

"Wait." Hollan looked up at Jacob. "You said the other day that the cabin looked like someone had been there."

"That would have been me," Gunter interrupted. "I cleaned it up and took shelter from a storm a short while back."

"I remember now." Hollan looked at her father. "You were gone all day, and I was so worried. If only I'd known then what the coming days would bring."

"Speaking of. . .we do need to move on," Jacob prompted.

Gunter stood to lead the way.

Jacob held Hollan back. "How long has it been since your vision returned? Since the day we walked around the island?"

"Before that." She frowned. "It was better when I woke up after hitting my head in the storm. I could see, but I wasn't sure my vision would stay."

"And you kept that from me? Why?" Jacob could hear the tremor in his voice. He wanted his wife to trust him, but apparently, after all he'd done in the past, she still didn't.

Hollan stared into his eyes. "I was afraid you'd think I didn't need you anymore. I was afraid you'd leave."

"So you trust me that little, even after I've told you repeatedly that I was here to stay."

"You did tell me that." Hollan nodded. "But that was when you thought I couldn't see. I wasn't sure things would stay the same if you knew. I needed more time."

"And when were you going to tell me?"

"The morning I was kidnapped."

"I see." Jacob stared back at her for a moment and then turned to stalk away up the path.

"That's it?" Hollan hurried to catch up with him. She grabbed his arm. "That's all you have to say?"

"I married you the moment I heard you were in need of a husband, Hollan. I stood by you through the hurricane, and I tended your injuries. I saved you from a ship full of rogues. If you don't trust me by now, after everything we've been through, I'm not sure I'll ever be able to regain your confidence."

twelve

"Jacob, wait!" Hollan's heart moved into her throat. She couldn't breathe. Her worst nightmare was coming true. Her deception had caused the exact scenario she'd wanted to avoid. She'd hurt Jacob, and now he didn't want to talk to her. "You kept saying you were here for me and that you wouldn't leave. But I wasn't sure if it was because you wanted to be here or because you had no choice."

"Not now, Hollan." Jacob continued to move ahead at a quick pace.

Hollan raised her voice. "I was afraid you'd leave if you knew I could see."

"I said not now." Jacob's words were clipped and cold.

Hollan dropped back and lagged behind. She could hardly see past her tears. She tried to tell herself it didn't matter, that with the return of her vision she'd be fine. She had her father back, and things could return to the way they'd been before this all happened. At least life would return to normal as soon as they figured out a way to rid themselves of David and his crew.

Hollan realized Jacob was right in that respect. This wasn't the time to worry about anything but their safety. They'd figure the rest out later. Even though she knew this all to be true, tears still forged their way down her cheeks.

The trio worked their way up the path, and Hollan wished for her boots. Chipped and broken shells lined the creek's bed, and the path wasn't any better. Hollan knew a cut from one of the shells could cause a serious infection. But she

116

wasn't about to ask Jacob for his help. She hesitated and glanced around, trying to figure out a way to walk without causing injury or drawing Jacob's attention to her ineptness.

"Keep up, Hollan. We need to carry on."

Hollan snapped, "I have to find my way around the shells."

Jacob came back and abruptly swept her up into his arms. "You should have worn your boots."

"I'll try to remember that next time I walk the shore prior to getting unexpectedly kidnapped."

A vein throbbed in Jacob's throat, but he didn't comment further.

Still, her feet were scratched and sore by the time they reached the shack. Her tears of heartache had diminished, but the pain of Jacob's anger simmered under the surface.

Jacob set her down next to the small building in the clearing. Hollan wandered over to the edge of the stream and sat down, placing her sore feet in the cool water. She cupped some of the water into her hands to wash her face and scrubbed away all trace of her tears.

"I'm going inside to lie down." Her father's face was pale with exhaustion.

"I'll help you get settled." Hollan moved to stand, but her father waved her away.

"Let me be. I can manage to lie down without assistance. Rest your feet."

Jacob watched from a distance and waited until her father had entered the shack before coming up beside her. "You should have told me."

"About my feet or my vision?"

He squatted at her side. Hollan glanced up at him. The sun broke through the leaves, and one shaft highlighted the gold in his hair. His green eyes were lined with fatigue. "Both."

"I told you. I was going to tell you about my vision, but the crew got to me first."

"And your feet?"

"What good would it do to tell you? What could you have done? If I'd worn my boots, I wouldn't have had a problem. It was my problem alone to deal with, and my feet are fine." Her words sounded bitter, but he'd walked away from her. Why would she think to bother him with anything after that?

"To answer your second question, I would have done this"—his face took on a devious expression as he reached over and swept her up into his arms—"earlier than I did."

"Put me down!" she hissed while glancing at the shack.

"No."

"I'm a mess."

"You look fine to me."

"Then maybe we need to be concerned about *your* vision."

"My vision is fine."

"I just spent the night on a smelly ship."

"And you had a nice dunk in the water after. You look beautiful."

"*Beautiful?* My dress is torn and cut to pieces. My petticoats are in shreds. My feet are filthy, and my hair is a mess. How can you say such a thing?"

"I mean it. I went a lot of years without seeing you. I intend to enjoy every moment of seeing you now."

"You're finished being angry?"

"Do I look angry?" He raised his eyebrows up and down. "You aren't going to chase me away, Hollan."

Hollan rolled her eyes. "My father's going to come out and see us this way."

"Your father isn't coming out. He's exhausted." Jacob settled back against a tree with Hollan held securely in his arms. "And regardless, he's not going to take offense."

She laid her head on his shoulder and snuggled closer. Her

heart felt full. "I didn't expect you to carry me through the woods. My feet hurt, but I'm fine. I would have dealt with sore feet."

"That's what I've been trying to tell you all along. Nothing—no problem—is yours to deal with alone. Not anymore. You have me to lean on now. I didn't marry you because you were blind. I didn't marry you because I felt sorry for you or because I felt there was no other choice. I married you because I love you. We'd planned to marry before I left. The pieces fell together when I returned, and I felt marriage to you was what God had brought me back here for. I'll carry you through any situation I need to."

Hollan stared at her reflection in the creek, afraid to meet his eyes. She knew she'd burst into tears. The stress of the past two weeks was taking its toll. She was exhausted from lack of sleep the night before and the anxiety caused by their escape. Her mind was a muddled mess.

"You need to rest. You barely recuperated from the blow to your head before you were taken. I'm sure you didn't sleep well on the ship."

The compassion in his voice was her undoing. A sob racked her body.

Jacob stroked her back. "I'm sorry," he crooned into her hair. "I didn't mean to make things worse."

"You didn't make things worse." She didn't want to talk. She just let him hold her while she stared into the water. The reflection there confirmed what she already knew. Her hair was a mess; her dress was dirty and torn. She looked awful. She likely smelled worse, even with her dip.

"You've made things so much better," she whispered.

"I haven't seen you cry before now."

"I haven't faced the reality of losing you before now."

He tilted her chin up. "I'm not leaving."

"You were so angry."

"Not angry, just frustrated."

His emerald eyes were so beautiful. He studied her.

"I don't want to make you frustrated."

He grinned. She'd forgotten about the way his dimples curved around his smile. "You've been making me frustrated since we were very young. I doubt anything's going to change in that respect."

"Oh."

He reached up to caress a strand of her hair.

She made a face and tried to swat him away.

His hand drifted down to her chin, and his thumb caressed her cheek. "Hollan, I'm going to disappoint you. You're going to frustrate me. But none of that will change the fact that we'll always love each other. Can you live with that?"

"I can," she whispered.

He slid his hand back to comb through her hair. He gently tugged her toward him as he leaned in for a kiss. "I can, too, very happily."

They sat forehead to forehead.

She breathed him in. "I'm so glad you're back."

"Me, too." He kissed her again and pulled away. "You need to rest."

"Don't leave."

He set her aside and tried to stand. She tugged him back down and leaned against him. He stroked her hair.

"I have to leave. Samson must be going nuts in the cottage. If the men come ashore—and I'm sure they will—the cottage will be their first target. I need to get Sam out of there and salvage some of our things."

"Poor Samson. I wondered how you got away without him."

"I had to lock him up." He seemed as hesitant about leaving as she was about watching him go. "Anyway, we need some supplies. I'll run up to the cottage and bring Samson back with me. We'll need food and clean clothes." He sent her a pointed look. "And I'll grab your boots and some more salve, too."

She laughed. She wanted to go with him, but no way would her feet allow that. Nor would Jacob. The brambles in the path would tear her to shreds. "Thank you. I appreciate your consideration. Just stay safe and hurry back quickly."

"I'll always hurry back to you."

Hollan could only nod.

"Do you want me to help you into the shack?"

"I'll stay out here, thank you. I'll have enough of the cabin when we have to go in there at dark."

"I'll hold you close and keep you safe."

Hollan blushed. "I'm sure you will. And my father will be right there on the other side, with me sandwiched in between. Sounds like a wonderful way to spend the night."

"Oh yeah, I suppose your father will be right there." Jacob's laugh told her he hadn't forgotten her father. He was teasing her again. "But we will make an excellent shield for you, protecting you from all that lurks in the dark."

Hollan shivered. "And there could be plenty of things lurking with David's crew wandering about."

"Last time we were here, you were worried about gators and snakes. Are you sure you don't want to go in with your father?"

"It was dark and creepy that day if I remember correctly, or at least it seemed so back then. Now I know scarier things lurk in the area. Today the clearing feels brighter and sun-dappled. I'll stay here."

"Sun-dappled?"

"Sun-dappled."

Jacob walked over to where he'd placed his coat and folded it into a square. He placed it on the ground and motioned for her to lie down. "Go to sleep. When you wake up, I'll be here."

"Sounds nice," she murmured. She was already drifting off.

⁂

Jacob hurried back to the cottage and heard Samson barking frantically from inside. He released the dog, and Samson ran in circles around his legs.

"She's fine, boy. I have her safely stashed away. We need to get you to safety as well."

Jacob hurried inside to gather some clothes for Hollan and her father. He stuffed a day's worth of food into the bag, too. He quickly grabbed anything he found of value and took it all to his room in the base of the lighthouse. Larger, less expensive items he hid as best he could in the outbuilding. He kept Gunter's rifle and ammunition with him.

"C'mon, boy, I need to make one more stop by the lighthouse before I take you to Hollan."

Samson didn't need any encouragement.

Jacob hurried back into his room and added his clothes to the bag. He hefted it up and placed it outside.

"Stay." He pointed to the bag, and Samson sat beside it. "I'll only be a moment."

He'd come a long way since the day he'd watched the men take Hollan. He was back at the lighthouse. At least now he had Hollan safely tucked away and out of the grasp of David. Still, he needed to get back to her.

Jacob hurried up the stairs. The lighthouse gave him a full view of the stranded ship. The ship didn't list quite as badly and seemed to have stabilized, but it remained stuck on the sandbar. Perhaps his wife had done her job a bit too well.

He noticed the smaller boats from the ship were being lowered to the water. He searched the treetops for any sign of the shack, but it couldn't be found. They'd be safe as long as they could get to Fletcher before David and his crew got to them.

Jacob secured the lighthouse as well as he could and motioned for Samson to come. He didn't think the men would carry along the right tools to break into the tower, and he hid any of Gunter's tools he could find. He prayed the men would be too tired to try to gain entry to the lighthouse. The damage they could do in vengeance would be expensive to repair.

Jacob and Samson set off for the shack. They finally arrived, with Samson leading the way through the trees, into the small clearing. Hollan lay where Jacob had left her. He quietly opened the door to the shack and placed their supplies inside. Gunter's exhausted snores reverberated throughout the room.

Jacob closed the door and walked over to where Samson stood watch over Hollan. "I can take care of things from here, boy." He dropped down beside Hollan and pulled her close. He shut his eyes and listened to her breathe.

She shifted in his arms. "Jacob?"

"I told you I'd be back."

"I'm glad."

Samson nudged his way between them. Hollan laughed and petted him.

"I think I got everything we need."

"Good." She nestled against Jacob, still half asleep.

Jacob grinned.

"I think nothing short of the arrival of outlaws would wake you up right now."

Her auburn hair fell across her face, and he pushed it back. She squinted up at him, her brown eyes warm. "I'm awake."

"Ah, then you still must consider me an outlaw."

"Hardly." She tried to sit up. "More like a hero."

"Stay. We have nowhere to go." He captured her with his arm. "So I'm a hero now. I like that much better than being compared to my outlaw family."

"I apologize for that."

"You had reason to be upset."

"Perhaps just a bit of a reason." She changed the subject. "And what did my hero find out through his explorations?"

"The crew is just now leaving the ship." He felt her tense up. "They won't find us here. I knew where to look and couldn't see a thing. It'll be dusk before they reach the lighthouse. I'm pretty sure they'll head to the cottage for now. While I was up in the lighthouse, I tracked the path Fletcher's boat will travel if he shows up tomorrow. If they leave a man on watch, he'll see Fletcher coming this way."

"From the lighthouse?"

"Only if they can gain entry. I'm hoping they're too tired to try."

Jacob had left his hair down, and Hollan absentmindedly stroked it as she listened. Her touch made it hard to concentrate.

"We'll need to warn Fletcher."

"Yes. I figure if we can get an early start in the morning and stick close to the trees, we can intercept Fletcher before he makes it as far as the ship. We can hop aboard the supply boat and be out of here before David and his men get off the dune."

"That sounds fine."

He leaned on his lower arm, put his other hand against his heart, and feigned surprise. " 'That sounds fine'?" he mimicked. "You don't want to add to the plan or take something away?"

"Very funny." She pushed him back down and laid her head on his chest. Samson wiggled closer. "I trust you."

"You do?" Jacob sat halfway up again. "You trust me completely this time?"

"I do. We've been through a lot during the past week, and you've stuck by me through it all. You didn't have to risk your life to rescue me, but you did. I do trust you."

"Thank you, Hollan. Your trust means everything to me. I'll never break that trust again."

She settled back against him just as Samson let out a low growl.

Jacob glanced at him and saw the hair raised on the back of the dog's neck. The dog growled again.

A gravelly voice sounded from behind them. "What do we have here?"

thirteen

Samson barked.

"Samson, it's just Papa." Hollan laughed. "Your sudden appearance and hoarse voice must have startled him, Papa."

Samson jumped to his feet and wagged his tail as he sheepishly hurried over to his master.

Hollan surveyed her father. "Are you feeling better?"

He definitely looked better now that he'd had some sleep.

"I feel much better."

"Good." Hollan turned to Jacob. "You said you brought more of our clothes back with you?"

"They're in the shack." Jacob's voice was groggy. He hadn't moved from his place on the ground.

"I think I'll go a ways up the stream to bathe and change."

"Don't go far," Jacob warned. He yawned. "I'll rest while you're gone."

"Stay within calling range, Hollan." Her father's face creased with worry. "The men might come ashore."

"I'll be close by, Papa."

"Actually, I think I'll tag along and freshen up myself. That way I'll be nearby if you need me."

Hollan rolled her eyes. She might be a married woman now, but her father apparently didn't see her as such. "As you wish, Papa."

She knew he'd worry the whole time she was gone if he didn't accompany her. And truth be told, she didn't want her father far away after being apart from him in such a way.

They gathered their supplies and walked up the overgrown

path. Hollan stopped and pointed out a small pool in the creek. "This looks like a perfect place. I'll stay here."

"Good. You'll be protected and safe. No one can get through this foliage. Jacob is just down the path behind us. And I'll go a bit ahead and stand guard from that angle."

"Thank you, Papa." She stopped and handed him a bar of lye soap. "I'm sure you can use some freshening up, too. You were on that ship longer than I."

"I can't wait to get in the water and then put on some fresh clothes. If we could light a fire, I'd burn these."

"Burying them will do just as well," Hollan teased.

Her father walked off, and Hollan savored the time alone. She slipped into the cool water and lathered up her hair. She scrubbed her body twice, just to make sure the filth of the ship was gone from her skin. Her skin tingled when she exited the water and dressed in fresh clothes.

She leaned back against a sun-warmed rock and contemplated the past few days while she waited for her father. She had her father back. The thought made her smile. More surprisingly, she had Jacob back. And for the first time, she felt confident that he meant it when he said he'd stay. He'd changed a lot during the past three years. They still needed to talk about why he'd left her in the first place. And she needed her father's explanation about what had happened to her mother.

The warmth of the late afternoon sun lulled her into a drowsy state. She listened to the sound of the birds in the trees. The wind rustled through the bushes. At least, Hollan hoped it was the wind. She knew the gators came out at dusk and willed her father to hurry.

She heard footsteps along the path and shrank down behind the rock.

"Hollan?"

"Papa? Oh, I'm glad you came back."

"Did something happen?" He glanced around.

"No." She smiled. "I'm just hearing things in the scrub. I'm ready to head back to Jacob. I don't want to meet up with an alligator any more than I want to meet up with David and his men."

Jacob woke up as they neared the small clearing and rubbed his eyes. "Is everything okay?"

"Just fine." Hollan smoothed her clean pink skirt and settled down beside him. He studied her fresh-scrubbed appearance. She couldn't help teasing him. "Everything meet your approval?"

"Indeed." He grinned. "I'm trying to figure out if you're the same woman who walked away from here a short while back."

"One and the same."

"I think I'd better follow suit." He hopped up to his feet. "Stay close to your father."

"You stay close to shore and make sure to be careful."

"What's the matter? You don't want me to end up as gator bait?"

She shuddered. "That's not exactly something to joke about."

"We have a bit of daylight left. I'll be fine."

"See that you are. I have some questions to ask when you return."

"Sounds serious."

"Maybe. But it's a conversation that's been a long time in coming."

"You're right." He nodded. "It has. We'll talk when I get back." He gathered his clothes and walked up the path from where they'd just come.

Hollan bent down and busied herself with cleaning and wrapping her sore feet.

"We need to talk, too, Hollan. Now's as good a time as any."

Hollan glanced back at her father. "About Mama?"

"Yes." He eased himself down beside her. "The night she—fell—from the lighthouse, something happened. Something bad."

"You don't have to tell me, Papa."

"I want to tell you. You need to know. You need to understand that she didn't do what she did to hurt you. She was hurting so badly, I don't think she gave anything else much thought."

"She'd just left the cottage. What could have happened?"

"David waited just outside, and he grabbed her. . . ." Her father stopped, his face both pained and angry.

"Papa, you don't have to do this."

"Yes, I do." He waved her words away. "David grabbed her, and he abused her. He—hurt—your mother. He violated her body. I was so close by, but I had no idea."

"Oh, Papa. I had no idea, either."

"She didn't want you to know." He shook his head. "I was supposed to watch out for her, but I wasn't there for her in her time of greatest need."

"You didn't know."

"That doesn't change things in my mind."

"What happened next?"

"I went into a rage. I told her to go back inside, and I went after the vile man."

"But you didn't find him?"

"No. And I heard you calling, and I was afraid for you."

"Why would David want to hurt Mama?"

"I don't know. I'll never know. He and his brothers and their father hurt a lot of people that night, for no reason anyone has ever been able to figure out."

"I know what happened." Jacob stood at the edge of the

path, his voice tortured. "I think I'm starting to understand."

They both spun around to look at him. He dropped his things beside the door of the shack and walked closer.

He sank down beside Hollan and took her hand. "He'd come to hurt you."

"But why? I didn't even really know him. Why would he want to hurt me?"

"Because hurting you would be the best way to hurt me." Jacob shook his head. "David hated that I was different from him and our father. He constantly goaded me and tried to get me to go along with them as they destroyed everyone in their path. I wouldn't have any part of it, and I spent most of my time with your uncle and aunt."

"I knew your family was rough, but I had no idea they were that bad."

"I didn't want you to know."

"Oh."

"You were my refuge. You were the bright spot in my life. I didn't want to dirty that up with my family's reputation."

"It wouldn't have changed anything between us."

"I know. I just didn't want to sully what we had when we were together. Regardless, things weren't good at home. That last night, they'd decided to skip town. The law was coming down on them, and they knew it was time to move on. I heard them talking and planning. David asked me to go along, and I refused. I tried to talk them out of it, and I tried to tell them about my beliefs. I told them it wasn't too late to start fresh. David laughed in my face. They didn't want anything to do with any of it. I said I didn't want anything to do with their deeds. I had you, and I had my life there in town. I had no reason to run."

Hollan saw the muscle working in Jacob's jaw. "What happened next?"

He struggled for control. "David said he was going after you, that maybe he'd just take you with him instead. He hated that he couldn't control me. He hated that I was so different. He wanted to be in control of everything."

"Oh, Jacob." Hollan tried to grasp everything he was telling her. The raw emotion on his face clearly showed his pain. "What did you do?"

"I went into a rage, just like your father did later. I'm not proud of the fact. David has a tendency to bring out the worst in a man."

"But I don't blame you. You were totally justified."

"David laughed and said he didn't really want to take you with them. . .he'd just take what he wanted from you and would leave it at that."

He looked at her. Hollan continued to hold his arm.

"I went after David. All three of them, my dad and my other two brothers, jumped me while David hit me from behind."

Hollan closed her eyes against the horrific image of Jacob being held by his own father and brothers while another brother attacked him. "That's atrocious."

"They knocked me unconscious." He blew out a breath. "When I woke up, your uncle was bent over me and they were gone. It was daylight. My head was pretty messed up. I croaked out your name and your uncle said you'd been traumatized and it would be best if I left you alone for a bit."

He threw a small stone into the creek and watched the water ripple out from where it landed. Hollan remained quiet, figuring he needed time to gather his thoughts before continuing.

"I figured—based on his comment—that David had succeeded in getting what he was after. I figured your uncle's phrasing was his way of telling me to leave you alone."

"So you just left?"

"No, I couldn't travel. I was in and out of consciousness for a few more days, and your aunt and uncle cared for me. When I was finally well, I asked about you again."

He shrugged. "Your uncle again repeated that you needed some time. You'd been injured. The whole town had been wronged. I had to go after my brothers. I couldn't let them get away with what they'd done."

"I had been injured. Just not as you thought. The weather was awful, and my mother was standing at the edge of the platform on top of the lighthouse. I was afraid she'd fall. I tried to take hold of her arm, to pull her back, but she just shook me away like I didn't matter. I fell and hit my head. When I woke up, I couldn't see. We hoped it would only be for a short time, that maybe it was caused from the trauma of everything that happened, but after several days passed. . .we had to accept that the loss of vision might be permanent."

"I'm so sorry."

Hollan nodded. "What happened after my uncle told you I still needed time?"

"I decided I'd go after my father and brothers. I wanted to find my own justice."

"But you didn't. You went to the law."

"You're right, I did. As I rode after them, God shook some sense into me. He placed some good people in my path. I decided I would bring them to justice, but I'd do it the right way. I didn't want to become like them."

Hollan's voice was soft. "So, you didn't leave me because you didn't want me. You left because you thought you'd lost me."

"Exactly." He took her hand in his. "I never stopped loving you, Hollan. I just thought I'd lost you because of what my brother did. I thought when your uncle said to give you time, you didn't want to see me again."

"But David never came to me...."

Her father spoke up. "Yes, he did."

Hollan was bewildered. "No, he didn't—"

"But he did...."

She glanced back and forth between them. Realization dawned. Her breath hitched. "He got Mama instead."

Her father nodded.

"Mama wasn't his intended victim. He thought she was me. Then it was my fault David hurt her."

Jacob pulled her close. "No, it wasn't your fault at all."

She pushed him away. "It was! He'd come for me. Mama went out there...."

"And in the storm, she looked so much like you that David mistook her for you." Her father nodded again. "Hollan, your mother wouldn't have had it any other way. She told me as much. She said he kept saying your name, even as she fought him. She said she was glad it was her he'd found, not you. She didn't blame you, and you can't blame yourself."

Horrified tears poured down Hollan's cheeks. "Then why did she do what she did?"

"I don't know. She was hurt, angry, devastated. She begged me not to go after him. Not with the rage I was in. If I'd only stayed with her..."

"You can't blame yourself, either, Papa." Hollan reached up to wipe her tears, but Jacob got to them first.

"Hollan, I don't think she jumped of her own free will. Now that we've all shared our views of that night, I think your mother must have gone up to the top of the lighthouse to get away from everything, to feel safe. You were in the cottage. She wouldn't want you to see how distraught she was. Your mother didn't leave you intentionally."

"I think you may be right." Hollan nodded slowly. She

turned to her father. "Papa, if you won't let me blame myself, you can't take that blame either."

"None of us are to blame. It took me three years to realize that." Jacob caressed her fingers with his thumb. His golden hair glistened. He surveyed her, looking deep into her eyes. She couldn't pull her gaze away from his. "Only God can judge them for their sins. The law can try them for their crimes. Our responsibility is to forgive."

"It's hard."

"It is, but if you don't forgive. . .if you hold the anger and bitterness in. . .you'll become just like them. Don't let them win."

She turned to her father. "Papa?"

"Your husband is right, Hollan. As hard as it is to hear, Jacob speaks the truth. David needs to be brought to justice, but as soon as that's accomplished, we need to go on with our lives. We need to move forward. God has blessed us through all this."

"I guess He has, hasn't He? I'll still have to work through the anger toward David, but God restored my vision. He brought Jacob back to me." She smiled up at him.

"He led me back to you," Jacob agreed.

"And He allowed you both to find me," her father added.

"So we're all in agreement." Hollan stared back and forth between both men. "But what now? How do we bring David to justice?"

Her father considered her question. "We leave first thing in the morning and intercept Fletcher."

"What if he can't make it? What if he can't get away? The hurricane might have caused a lot of damage."

Jacob surveyed her expression. "You have something on your mind."

"Yes." She raised an eyebrow. "I do."

"I'm afraid to ask. . .but. . ." Her father's blue eyes twinkled. "Are you gonna fill us in?"

"David and his crew rowed ashore to get over here, right?"

"Right."

"They'd have to leave their boats onshore, wouldn't they?"

"I believe they would."

Jacob exchanged a look with her father. "Are you thinking what I'm thinking?"

Her father nodded. "I'm pretty sure I am."

They both looked back at her.

Jacob spoke first. "If they did leave the boats onshore, they'd surely have a guard."

"Guards can be bribed." Hollan shrugged. "Or overthrown."

Jacob laughed. "You say that like it's such a simple thing. And you're volunteering us for the job?"

"I'll do my part." Hollan tipped up her chin and dared him to cut her out of the plans.

"What did you have in mind?"

"I could sashay over and distract whoever it is while you two strike from behind."

"My wife is villainous!"

Hollan snorted. "I'm not. I'm just willing to do whatever needs to be done."

Gunter sat in contemplative silence.

"Papa?"

"I don't want to use you as bait. These men are very dangerous. Now they're both dangerous and angry."

"Do you have a better plan?"

"Well, I don't as of now, but I bet we can come up with one before dawn."

Jacob leaned forward and rested his arm on his knee. "They'll be watching for us. If we leave before daybreak, we'll have a better chance of getting away."

Hollan grabbed his sleeve. "And if we catch them off guard, maybe we can just slip away with one of the boats. David didn't seem to hire the brightest of men for his crew."

"That's because anyone with a lick of sense would have stayed far away from him."

"Jonathon actually has a heart," Hollan disagreed. "I don't know why he's with them."

They sat in silence for a few minutes.

"Jacob. . .Papa. . ."

Both men answered in unison. "What?"

"What if Jonathon volunteered for the watch?"

Jacob thought for a moment. "The odds are against that, Hollan."

"I know. But just think. God has protected us so far. What if He's put the next step into place by giving us Jonathon as a guard?"

"It could happen. And if not, I'm sure He has a plan for us to get out of here to safety."

"We won't know until we get there."

"You want to go now?"

"Why not? What better time? We've all slept. We'll sleep better if we get to the mainland. They won't expect us to act until morning. And they have to be exhausted, too. They worked hard all day trying to unload the ship. David told me he wanted to go up the inland canal because officials were looking for him. He won't want to stay around very long."

Gunter exchanged a look with Jacob. "I think the lady is on to something."

She smiled with relief. "So we act tonight? Now? I think I'll go crazy if we have to sit here any longer."

"You'll be okay walking through the area in the dark? I know you aren't real fond of it here, even in the daylight."

"I'm fonder of the thought of walking away than I am of spending the night here in that shack. And I have my boots on this time."

Jacob stood and pulled her to her feet. She dusted off her skirt. Gunter joined them.

"Let's get something to eat then see what the shoreline holds."

fourteen

The moon barely provided enough light through all the foliage for them to see as they walked down the overgrown path. Hollan stayed close to Jacob and clutched the hem of his shirt. Gunter followed close behind.

They neared the shore and walked quietly along the trees. Even Samson seemed to understand the gravity of the situation as he kept pace beside Hollan. She appreciated the solid warmth of his body as he pressed against her leg. She kept a firm hand on the nape of his neck. If anything lurked in the bushes, Samson would warn them in plenty of time.

They'd debated leaving him behind, but with no way to secure the shack's door, he'd break free and end up tagging along anyway. At least this way they had a semblance of control over the situation.

The large outline of David's ship loomed high against the horizon, its features eerie in the moonlight. The smaller boats were pulled up on shore, just as they'd hoped, and Hollan didn't see any sign of a watchman.

"No one seems to be around," Hollan whispered. "Maybe they're so cocky they don't expect us to steal—I mean, borrow—one."

"If so, it's more likely they were too tired or too drunk and they didn't give it a thought," Jacob interjected.

"Perhaps it's a mixture of both," her father agreed.

Jacob glanced back at Hollan, the moonlight highlighting the smirk on his face. "And surely my dear brother wouldn't have an issue with us borrowing one of his boats."

"Yes, he's so accommodating and thoughtful." The sarcasm rolled off Hollan's tongue.

They huddled at the edge of the trees.

"I've been wondering. How *did* David get a boat so quickly?" Hollan asked. "If you followed him here. . . ?"

"I told you I had to argue with God a bit before I headed back. David had time to secure the vessel. As to how, I'm sure it wasn't by legal means. The crew might belong to the ship—and it's a skeleton crew at that—but I doubt the ship belongs to my brother."

"Well said." Hollan was ready to leave the island. "Let's keep going."

They slowly crept along the edge of the curved beach that contained the rowboats. "If no one is here, we'll just hop in and go, is that the plan?" Hollan asked. "The area appears to be deserted." She couldn't wait to get out of there.

Samson let out a low growl.

"Then again, we could be wrong," Hollan hissed as the dark form of a man rose up from where he'd apparently been sleeping on the bottom of one of the boats.

They all ducked in unison.

"Who's out there?"

"It's Jonathon!" Hollan whispered, then stood and started to answer.

Jacob yanked her back down and shook his head then put a finger to his lips. Hollan nodded.

"We need to make sure he's alone."

"Of course. I'm sorry."

They waited in silence. No one else moved or answered. Jonathon stood and stepped out of the beached boat and headed for the trees. Samson growled again, and Hollan returned her hand to the nape of his neck.

"He's coming this way!" she hissed.

Jacob held up a hand. Hollan quieted. Her heart beat quickly in her chest as she watched her husband's actions. He crouched in the shadows and followed Jonathon's movements with scrutinizing eyes.

When Jonathon stood within reach of them, Jacob lunged forward and grabbed the man around the neck. He pulled him close against his chest.

"Jonathon. Don't make a sound. Is there anyone else here with you?" Jacob asked in a quiet voice.

"No, I'm in charge of the boats." Jonathon sounded rattled.

Hollan's heart went out to the man. "It's okay, Jonathon. It's just us."

Jacob loosened his grip, but Jonathon didn't move.

"You shouldn't oughta sneak up on a man like that," he groused. "A man could drop dead from fright. I didn't want to stay out here in the first place. It's spooky."

"Says the man who kidnapped me from a beach," Hollan pointed out.

"Fair enough." Jonathon shifted on his feet. He didn't exude any of the cockiness that David liked to portray. "I do apologize for that. But I couldn't go against the other men. They'd have killed me on the spot."

"I'm glad they didn't." Hollan's voice softened. She didn't blame Jonathon for not helping. But she did hope he'd help them now. "You can make it up to me, though."

"How's that?" His voice held a hint of distrust.

"You can let us have a boat, let us get away."

"Oh, I don't know. David would be so angry."

"Then go with us. We'll take you to safety."

"I don't think there's a place safe enough to get away from David."

"If we can get to the authorities, David will be captured by the law. You'll be safe. Think about it, Jonathon! Won't you feel good knowing you're on the right side of the law for a change?"

"I ain't never been on that side that I can remember. . . ." Jonathon sounded dubious.

"Jonathon. God put you here to help us. I'm sure of it. If you help us, we can help you."

"No offense, ma'am, but David's the one who put me here, not God."

"That's how it might look to you"—Hollan reached for his arm—"but I feel sure God put you here to help us. We can help each other. Come with us, help us paddle through the channel, and we'll hide you in a safe place when we get to town."

"I didn't know there was a town nearby."

"It isn't exactly a town, per se, but there's a small church and a building that's used as a general store. There's an acting sheriff. The townsfolk look out for each other. You'd be welcome there."

He hesitated.

"You don't want to let God down, do you? We need you to help us."

"You're sure I'll be safe?"

"Yes. But we need to leave right now."

"On the open water, at night? With a woman on board?"

"You can't possibly still blame *me* for all the problems after you kidnapped me. There's no such thing as bad luck. Everything that happened to you, Paxton, and Nate was caused by your own actions. And as for nighttime travel, there's enough moonlight to see pretty well. We know the waters, and this stretch won't be difficult at all. It's just a little ways away."

Jonathon didn't answer. Hollan didn't know what they'd do if he refused. She didn't want to see the man hurt and didn't know that Jacob and her father even had it in them to hurt a man. She had a feeling, though, that if pushed into a corner, when it came to her safety against Jonathon's, Jacob's protective instinct would kick in.

"Please? This would more than make up for the kidnapping." Hollan prayed for the right words. "If you help us escape now, the law will see that you assisted us. Otherwise, you might be charged with kidnapping along with the others when they're caught. And they will be caught, if not right now, then soon. David said the officials were after him."

"You're sure we'll get away?"

"Do you expect David or any of his men to come check on you tonight?"

"No, they won't be coming around till morning."

"Then we need to go now."

Jonathon nodded and led the way to the farthest boat. "If they catch us, I'll tell them you threatened me with that shotgun Jacob's carrying."

"Nice to know you have our backs," Hollan muttered.

Jacob bent down to help push the boat into the water. "I don't intend to let them catch us."

Hollan settled into the seat at the bow, the same place she'd sat when David's men first took her from shore. She patted the seat and with a whine Samson climbed in with her. He settled at Hollan's feet on the floor.

Jacob and Gunter took the middle seat, and Jonathon took the rear.

"Wait," Hollan hissed. "What about the men in the hold?"

"None of them made it," Jonathon said. "If it makes you feel better, they weren't much better than David and his crew. They were privateers during and after the war."

Hollan shuddered. "I'm not sure that makes me feel better, but thank you."

"Hollan, you'll have to watch for debris and sandbars," Jacob instructed. "We'll stay close to shore, but you'll have to guide us if you see anything coming our way."

Hollan shifted in her seat so she could see where they were going.

They traveled slowly. The gentle current worked with them. Hollan was glad Jonathon had come along. Though he wasn't a large man, he was burly, and his added strength as they rowed didn't hurt as they made progress.

"I have a confession to make." Jonathon's hesitant voice sounded loud in the silence. He laid his oar across his lap.

Jacob and her father stopped rowing, but they continued to drift along. They all stared at the man as they waited.

"We ran into a man on our way over this afternoon."

A chill passed through Hollan. "A man?"

"Yes. He came across on a flatboat just as we neared your island in our rowboats."

"A flatboat. . .like a supply boat?"

"Yes'm." Jonathon shifted nervously in his seat and set the boat to rocking.

"Sit still!" Jacob commanded. "What happened to this man?"

"David. . .um. . .well, he and some of the men sort of took advantage of him."

"Took advantage?" Hollan asked, confused.

"They beat him and stole his load from the boat."

Hollan's heart pounded. "Where is he?"

"I don't know. After stealing the supplies, they left him aboard his boat and sent it downstream. Last I saw him, the supply boat was floating this way."

"If the current caught Fletcher, he could be well on his way out to sea." The anger in Jacob's voice was palpable.

"I didn't do it," Jonathon defended.

"You might as well have if you just stood by and let it happen," Jacob accused.

Jonathon looked down and didn't say anything more.

Jacob ran a hand through his golden hair. "I'm sorry. You didn't have a choice. They would have just beaten you and added you to the boat with Fletcher or worse."

"We need to find him." Her father's voice was full of resolve. His comment was a command.

"We need to get closer to the other side. We've been fighting the same current his boat would have. It keeps pushing us to the east. The shapes of the vessels are different, so his boat would have flowed more smoothly across the water. There's a chance we'll pass him on the far side."

"If he didn't capsize or fall off."

"He was pretty well centered when they sent his boat off," Jonathon said quietly.

They crossed the channel and headed toward land. Hollan felt vulnerable out in the open, even though she knew no one could possibly be nearby. The moon glistened off the top of the water. She prayed Fletcher would be all right and that they would find him.

Though Hollan longed to dangle her fingers in the water, she knew better than to do it at night. She rested her elbow on her knee and put her chin on her fist as she watched the water for obstacles. She searched the shore for any sign of the supply boat. The lateness of the hour caught up with her, and she struggled to stay awake.

Lord, help me to focus and do my part. I'm so tired. I don't want to let the men down or fall asleep in my seat.

Just as she finished the prayer, a large shape rose up from the water and then rolled back down in front of her. Hollan smiled. A dolphin! She hadn't seen one in three years, and here this one was swimming in front of them as if directing their boat across the waters. Any thoughts of sleep drifted away as she watched the magnificent creature. Each time he ducked below, she hoped he'd surface again. As long as she could see him, she'd know there wasn't anything in front of them.

Finally the dolphin did a half turn and swam away from the boat. Hollan wanted to beg him to return. But as she looked up, she noticed a structure ahead of them.

"I see the dock! And Fletcher's boat is there." Hollan all but bounced on her seat as they neared their destination.

"Sit still, girl, before you swamp us," her father's good-natured voice called from the middle seat. "Looks like Fletcher made it back."

"What a relief."

"Strange," Jonathon said. "It looked like they did him in."

"Fletcher is a very strong man. He must have recovered from the blows and made his way back home," Jacob stated.

"I sure hope so. I'd feel a lot better."

"We'll know soon. We'll check on him as soon as we get in." Jacob dragged his oar in the water, spinning them around. The current pushed them closer to shore.

"Now to see how the town has fared."

They pulled the boat up against the dock. Jacob jumped out to secure it. He helped Hollan from the boat, and the other two men joined them. Samson ran happily from one end of the dock to the other.

Fletcher's boat was tied securely to the pier. There was no sign of the man on the dock or in the water nearby.

"Where do we go from here?" Jonathon asked nervously.

"We don't have far to go," Hollan assured him. "We'll go to my uncle's house. It's just up the road from here."

"It's the middle of the night. Will he be upset to find all of us at his door?"

Hollan grimaced. "He's the reverend of the church. He's used to late-night calls."

They trudged along the sandy path, the moonlight leading

the way. Samson ran ahead. Every so often he'd return to check on them, and then off he'd go again. An alligator bellowed from the marsh to their right, and Hollan shivered. Jacob wrapped a reassuring arm around her shoulders.

Hollan let out a sigh of relief when they reached civilization, though the houses they passed were all dark. As they neared the row of buildings that composed the town, Jacob stopped. "I want to alert the sheriff. I doubt David would be so brass as to come here in the morning, but it's best not to take a chance."

"I'll head up the road. I'll wait for you there." Jonathon backed away.

"Nonsense." Hollan grabbed his arm. "You'll stay here with us."

She could feel his muscles tense when the sheriff opened the door.

"What's going on?" The gruff voice made her want to run, too, but she stood firm.

Jacob nodded toward Hollan. "Pastor Edward's niece here was kidnapped from the beach yesterday by my brother and his crew of men. They met with some misfortune and ran their boat ashore and have now moved into the cottage at the lighthouse."

"I see." The sheriff looked at each of them in turn. "Fletcher apparently met up with the same group on his way to your place. He made it back, but he's in pretty bad shape."

"Where is he?" Hollan asked.

"They took him to Doc when they first found him, but he's at his mother's now. We were going to put together a posse at first light and go over to check on you. At least now we can concentrate on the hurricane repairs. Where are you all headed?"

"We're headed for Edward's place, and we'll stay there for the night."

"I'll make sure to keep an eye out for anything suspicious."

"Thank you." Jacob reached out his hand, and the sheriff shook it. "When do you think you'll be able to secure the island? David said they were wanted. That's the reason he attempted the channel as it was."

"You said no one's in harm's way?"

"No, and David and his men aren't going anywhere fast. They're stuck there. Unless they decide to come over here."

"I'll set up watch, but I doubt David will come here. He's still a wanted man. We're still repairing damage from the storm. We need to secure the homes that are open to the elements. I'd guess we have about two to three more days, and then we'll gather up a posse."

"Three days?" Hollan asked in disbelief. "The cottage and lighthouse could be in shambles if you wait that long!"

"Hollan, it'll be fine." Her father laid a reassuring hand on her shoulder. "We're safe, and that's what matters most."

"What about the ships, Papa? Who will keep them safe? The lighthouse needs to guide them."

"Gunter? Is that you?" The sheriff leaned forward with his lantern.

"Yes, Sheriff Roberts, it's me."

"I'm glad to see you safe. Parson Edward said you were missing."

"David and his crew took me just before the storm hit. Hollan and Jacob came to my rescue."

"Only after they kidnapped me!" Hollan filled in. "But Jacob came for us both."

"I'm sorry this happened to you." The sheriff lifted his lantern and stared at Jonathon. "And who do we have here?"

"Jonathon, sir." Jonathon's voice quaked under the sheriff's perusal.

"That don't tell me much."

Hollan hurried to intervene. "He helped us escape. He's from the ship."

"Did you now? I'm glad to hear that. We'll need to talk in the morning. I'll have some questions for you."

"Yes, sir." Relief tinged Jonathon's words. "I'll be here."

Sheriff Roberts looked at Jacob. "Swan. It's good to have you home. Edward told me about the marriage. Congratulations to you both."

They thanked him.

"Go on with you now. We'll all get some sleep, and I'll see you in the morning."

They walked up the road toward Edward's place.

"Your uncle has room enough for all of us?" Jonathon asked.

"He does. He'll probably put you men up in the church, and I'll stay in their home."

"Will you be safe there?" Jonathon continued with his questions. "David is a dangerous man."

"Yes, she'll be safe," Jacob interrupted. "I intend to make sure of it."

"Jacob, you need to get some sleep. I'll be fine. David won't know where we are. He surely won't dare to come after us."

"I agree. Most likely he won't. But I'm not taking any chances. If I have to sit on Edward's front porch, I'll do so in order to know that you're safe."

"Then perhaps we'll all stay in their home. They have several extra rooms."

"We'll see what Edward says. But I can guarantee if you're staying in that house, I'll be right there with you."

Edward answered his door and welcomed them in. Ettie pulled Hollan into her arms and cried when she saw Gunter.

"My brother!" Edward's eyes moistened as he took in the sight of Gunter. "You're alive."

"I'm fine. Or I will be after a bit of rest."

"You look well, Hollan." Edward beamed. "Married life must agree with you."

Hollan smiled up at Jacob. "Much to my surprise, it does."

"And Jacob. Is island life everything you hoped it would be? Did you find it to be a balm to your weary soul?"

Hollan laughed out loud.

"You find the question amusing?" Her uncle looked confused.

Jacob looked at Hollan, and they shared another smile. "Life on the island has been interesting to say the least. Two things stand out at the moment, though. Hollan has her sight back, and Gunter is safe."

"Hollan!" Ettie's tears continued. "I'm so happy, sweetheart. Let me look at you."

"More importantly, Auntie, let *me* look at *you*."

"We have a lot to catch up on."

"Indeed we do."

Aunt Ettie turned to Hollan's father.

"Gunter"—she gave him a little poke—"you gave us all quite a scare."

Uncle Edward raised his hands. "I'm glad we've all had a moment to catch up, but I'm sure you didn't make your way out here in the middle of the night to share your good news."

fifteen

"Gunter and Hollan were kidnapped by my brother David." The words rolled off Jacob's tongue.

A vein in Edward's neck began to throb. "Hasn't that boy caused y'all enough grief?"

"He's hardly a boy anymore, Ed," Ettie corrected. "But he does need to be stopped."

"Where is he now?"

Hollan answered, "He's on the island."

"Then we need to go after him. I'll get the sheriff."

"We've already talked to the sheriff, Uncle Edward. We're meeting him again first thing in the morning."

"Hmmph."

"There's more." Hollan knew her uncle and aunt were very close to Fletcher and Sylvia. "Fletcher apparently brought our supplies over about the same time David and his men came ashore. They stole everything he had, beat him, and left him for dead."

"Oh dear me." Ettie's hand was at her throat, and she fanned herself.

"Now, dear, sit down before you get yourself too worked up." Uncle Edward helped her over to the settee. "Where's Fletcher now?"

Jacob shifted on his feet. He looked tired enough to fall over. "According to the sheriff, he's home with Sylvia. We intend to go out there in the morning, too."

"I'll be going with you." Edward sighed. "Ettie and I were at the Black place all day. We had no idea."

"Poor Sylvia, dealing with this all alone." Ettie kept shaking her head.

"She's a strong woman, Ettie. I'm sure she's fine."

Hollan listened to them talk. "Well, I'm glad Sylvia was here to care for Fletcher." A plan began to formulate in Hollan's mind. If the menfolk were too busy to go over and capture an outlaw, she'd talk to Sylvia about flushing them out somehow. Surely the woman would be just as incensed as Hollan after what happened to her son. "She has to be furious at David."

"As well she should be," Ettie huffed.

Ah, yes. Hollan would surely have an ally in Sylvia. Ettie was upset, and it wasn't even her son hurt, though Hollan was like a daughter to her.

The simple facts were her father wasn't well, the lighthouse was unattended, and local seafarers were unsafe as long as they had no light to guide them. Hollan glanced at her father. He'd paled and now looked exhausted. She hurried to his side. "Papa?"

"I'm just tired. I suppose all the excitement of the past few weeks is catching up with me."

"Well, let's get you tucked into bed, then." Ettie was on her feet and acting as hostess, leading the weary Gunter to a room at the back of the house. "And you two take the room upstairs across from ours—Hollan's room when she stays here," she called as she retreated down the hallway.

Hollan darted her eyes to Jacob.

"If you don't mind, I'd rather stay down here where I can watch the door. Let Hollan sleep in the bed. She needs a good night's sleep."

"As do you," Hollan quipped. "You've lost several nights' sleep."

"I'll be fine. Like I told you before, between the war and the traveling, I've learned to sleep in snatches."

"Jonathon." Ettie's no-nonsense voice as she came up the hall made the man jump. "You'll settle into the room across from Gunter. Follow me to the back of the house, and I'll show you the way."

Jonathon blushed. "Oh no, ma'am. I'll be fine on the porch or in a shed if you have one out back. I haven't slept on the likes of a bed in longer than I can remember."

"Then it's high time you had a good night's sleep. Tonight you'll be blessed with a bed."

"I've already been blessed in many ways tonight." Jonathon glanced at Hollan.

She smiled back at him. "You deserve it, Jonathon. You helped save us. Tomorrow I'll make a celebration breakfast in your honor."

"I'm not sure I earned such an honor."

"You've more than earned it, Jonathon," Hollan encouraged.

"You brought our niece home safe and sound. We will celebrate."

Jonathon beamed.

Edward walked with Ettie and Jonathon as they headed for the back of the house, leaving Hollan and Jacob temporarily alone.

"Thank you for volunteering to stand watch. That saved us an awkward situation."

"I volunteered to stand watch because I want to know you're safe. Otherwise I would have grabbed Ettie's suggestion before you could have said anything about it."

"Oh," Hollan croaked.

He stepped closer, and his green eyes stared into hers with such intensity she figured he could read her deepest thoughts. "And when we get this all taken care of, I expect to start all over with this marriage. This time we'll do it right."

"I see."

Jacob laughed. "My wife appears to be tongue-tied for the first time ever."

Hollan mashed the toe of her boot into a knothole on the floor. "And what am I to say to such talk? I wonder. . . ."

"What?"

"Would it be possible to have our wedding ceremony over?" She felt silly asking. "I'd love to have Aunt Ettie there this time around. And our friends. . ."

"If that's what it takes to set this marriage straight."

"Your intensity embarrasses me." Hollan stepped away but laughed. She might as well get used to it.

He moved closer still. "It isn't my intent to embarrass you. But you should know my thoughts. We'll start our marriage again, and we'll do it right this time."

"I'd like that."

"Good." He grinned. "Now get up to bed. We have a busy day tomorrow."

❧

Hollan woke later than she'd planned the next morning, after the long and tiring night. She couldn't wait to talk to Sylvia. She wanted to check on Fletcher. But she also wanted to ask for Sylvia's assistance in ridding their lives of David. If Jacob wouldn't go along with her, and the townsmen still wouldn't go after David after all that he'd done, she'd find a way to capture him herself. Surely after a night's sleep, Jacob, the sheriff, and the townspeople would agree this couldn't wait.

A few minutes later she listened as Jacob dashed her dreams of going home soon.

"We can't do this yet. The town needs to be secured, then we'll worry about the island. People will lose their life's belongings if we don't fix their roofs before the next storm rolls through."

"Jacob, why are you standing against me in this? Our life

has been in turmoil far too long and all because of David."

"I'm not standing against you, Hollan. But we need to have a plan. David's not going anywhere. The ship is stuck for now."

"But I want to go home. I want our life to get back to normal. I want to enjoy the return of my vision in the place I love."

"Oh. . .and here I thought you were in a hurry to get back so you could officially start your life with me."

Hollan blushed. "You know I want that, too. But first we need to rid the island of David."

Jacob refused to budge.

She tried her ace in the hole. "The lighthouse is unattended. At least, it's unattended if they haven't broken into it yet. They've probably destroyed everything I hold of value. I could lose everything I own, too."

"I admit that bothers me." Jacob paced as he always did when stressed. "But the lighthouse is well secured, and I'm pretty sure they won't be able to get in. I'll replace anything we lose."

"You're 'pretty sure' they won't get in?" Hollan raised an eyebrow. "Do you realize how long it will take to replace the lens if they find a way to damage it?"

The scent of fried ham and eggs wafted into the room from the kitchen. Hollan's mouth watered, momentarily distracting her.

"Hollan. We can't go back until we put a plan in place. Gunter, Jonathon, and I will talk to the sheriff as soon as we've eaten breakfast. I want you to stay here and wait with Ettie. Understand?"

"I need to go see Sylvia."

Jacob's face lit up. "That's a wonderful plan. You spend your time with Sylvia and Fletcher while we menfolk come up with our plan."

Hollan scowled.

Jonathon walked into the room. He looked uncomfortable. "Good morning."

"Is everything all right?" Hollan hurried over to his side.

"I'm not used to waking up in a—home. It's unnerving."

Hollan smiled at Jacob. "I'm sure it is. Aunt Ettie has breakfast ready, and we were just heading that way. Do you want to clean up and meet us in the kitchen?"

Jonathon nodded and shuffled toward the back of the house while Hollan and Jacob headed for the kitchen.

Hollan hesitated in the doorway. "Aunt Ettie? If you don't mind, I'd like to go on over and see how Sylvia and Fletcher fared last night."

"Before you eat?" Jacob frowned.

Her aunt looked up from the biscuits she was pulling from the oven. "Can't you wait, dear? I'd planned to walk over with you."

"Father needs someone here. I'll stay if you'd like. . . ." She made her voice wistful.

"But you'd really rather go yourself." She sighed. "I know how important Sylvia is to you. I'll stay here with Gunter. You go on ahead."

"If you're sure. . ."

"Go on. Here"—Aunt Ettie grabbed a biscuit and smeared it with jam—"at least eat this on the way."

Hollan took the biscuit and gave her aunt a grateful look. She glanced at Jacob and tried to hide the guilt she was sure he could read in her eyes. "I'll be going then. I'll see you. . .after?"

"After? Oh, right. We'll talk to the sheriff and meet up with you later." He shrugged, though he still looked perplexed. Or did he look suspicious?

Most likely Hollan was merely feeling guilty.

She headed out the door and up the sandy path. The late morning sun beat down upon her back, and the day promised to be clear. The marshes on either side of the road were bustling with activity. Butterflies flitted from plant to plant. A lizard darted across the path right in front of her. A bit farther Hollan saw a snake slither through the tall reeds at her side.

The lizards and butterflies didn't bother her, but after the snake sighting, Hollan picked up her pace. It took the better part of an hour before Sylvia's small cabin was just around the bend.

"Hollan! What a pleasant surprise." Sylvia had been sitting on her front porch, sipping from a steaming mug, but now she hurried to her feet. She tilted her head and studied Hollan for a moment.

Hollan stared back and grinned.

The wind blew Sylvia's hair. Suddenly her hand flew to her chest. "You can see again."

"Yes, I can see again." She smiled at her friend for a moment then sobered. "I heard about Fletcher. How's he doing?"

A cloud passed over Sylvia's face. "He'll be fine, no thanks to whoever harmed him. We were so worried about you."

"I'm fine. . .and I know who did this to him."

Sylvia slapped her mug down with a *thump*. "You tell me, and I'll go after them on my own!"

"You don't have to go alone. I'd love to go with you." Hollan walked up the steps and placed a hand on Sylvia's arm. "The man responsible for hurting Fletcher kidnapped my father and me. He's also responsible for what happened to my mother."

"What a horrid person. How do you know?"

Hollan told her friend what had happened.

"We must put a stop to this."

"I agree, but Jacob says the town isn't in any shape to help us out. And he's right. People need a roof over their heads before the next storm hits."

"But a very dangerous man is lurking out there, waiting to

hurt his next victim. We won't be safe until the authorities get him under control."

"I agree, but that isn't my only concern. The ships aren't safe without the lighthouse."

They exchanged a mischievous glance.

"Do you have a plan?" Sylvia took another sip from the mug. "You aren't thinking of going alone. . . ?"

"No—o—o," Hollan drawled. "But I *am* thinking of going over with help." She sent Sylvia a meaningful look.

"We don't want to put ourselves in danger."

"I know that island like the back of my hand."

"The menfolk will be so upset."

"I'm willing to take that chance. I'm pretty upset myself that we have to sit here and do nothing while those outlaws ruin what little I have left from my previous life."

"This isn't a decision to make lightly, dear."

"I'm not making it lightly." Hollan put her hands on her hips. "David has hurt too many people. If we don't act, someone else will be hurt. I saw the look in Jacob's eyes, Sylvia. He's telling me he has to wait to act, but I'm afraid he'll go alone and he'll confront David. I don't want him hurt on my behalf."

"Yet you're willing to be hurt on his behalf?"

"I don't intend to get hurt. But yes, I'd do anything for him. He's been here for me through everything we've endured of late. I owe him."

"But you don't think it'll upset him if something happens to you?"

"I don't intend for anything to happen to you or to me. I plan to use a little subterfuge. I'm not going to confront David."

Doubt crept across Sylvia's features. "Subterfuge?" She raised an eyebrow.

"I just want to set a bonfire as a warning to sailors entering the mouth of the river. We might not be able to use the lighthouse to show them the island's location, but we can light a huge fire on the beach that will serve the same purpose. They'll see the fire and know land is nearby."

"I don't know. Maybe we should just wait for the men to figure this out."

"And let Jacob sneak over on his own?" Hollan shook her head. "I won't chance that. We have to watch out for the sailors. At least help me set a warning fire on the shore. David said he and his crew are wanted. If men on ships are searching for them, I'd like to do my best to protect those men and lead them our way."

They stared at each other for a few more moments. Hollan prayed Sylvia would come along. "Please, Sylvia."

"Perhaps you just solved your own dilemma." Sylvia waved her hands and sighed. "I can't exactly sit by and let you do this alone."

"You're coming with me?"

"I suppose I am."

"And Fletcher will be all right if you leave him?"

"He'll be fine. He's sleeping. Let me run inside and make sure he has everything he needs. Then we'll make our plans. We don't want to get over there too early, either. We need to do this under the protection of dusk."

"Sylvia—"

"Yes?" Hollan's friend stopped and turned around.

"Thank you."

"Sweetheart, I don't want you to take responsibility for what we're about to do. I'm doing this for you, yes, but also for your mother, Fletcher, and myself. I'm doing this for all of us. I want the man responsible for hurting my son behind bars."

Hollan smiled. "I understand. And I intend to do my best to see that happen, too."

sixteen

"We need to put in here," Hollan whispered. "We don't want David's crew to see us if anyone's on watch."

"I hardly think you need to whisper, Hollan. We're in the middle of a marsh."

"Must you remind me?" Hollan shuddered. If the reeds, taller than their boat, didn't clue her in, the stench of the stagnant water surely did. "Maybe I'm whispering so the creatures don't know we're here. Maybe it has nothing to do with David and his men hearing us."

Sylvia laughed. Hollan's nerves were shot, and she said crazy things when she was stressed and tired.

They'd commandeered Fletcher's supply boat for the trip. Sylvia was accustomed to piloting the flat-bottomed boat. She felt it would allow them to skirt the shallower water and hug the shore more closely. It would also hold the most supplies. Sylvia had been right on every count. Hollan knew she'd made the right decision when she invited the woman along.

They worked together to guide the front of the boat alongside the shore around the bend from where David's men had placed their boats. The watery ground was marshy. Hollan pushed back her fears of snakes and alligators and maneuvered the flatboat deep into the swaying reeds and grasses. They were able to secure the boat mostly out of sight. Hollan jumped into the water, saturating her boots, and tied the vessel to a low-lying tree.

"Tie both ends of the boat securely, dear. Otherwise it will swing back and forth and might work its way loose. We don't want it to be damaged."

Hollan shuddered. "You're right. I want to be sure we have a way off this island."

After doing what Sylvia told her, Hollan helped the older woman off the boat. They gathered their supplies. Sylvia had prepared well for the expedition. They were stocked with weapons, food, and various types of gear, the use of which Hollan didn't even understand.

The sun sat low on the horizon.

"Tell me what you have planned before we leave here," Sylvia requested. "We might not be able to talk as freely later."

"Well, I'd hoped to be here much earlier than this. But since you and I wasted time chatting—"

"Planning and preparing, dear. That wasn't a waste of time."

"Whatever you want to call it, it set us way off track," Hollan replied.

"Not necessarily. The dusk will keep us covered. They're drinking men. They should be well into their indulgences by now."

Which will put us into even greater danger if we get caught. Hollan felt responsible for Sylvia's well-being. It was one thing to deal with evil men. It was another thing entirely to deal with drunken evil men.

Hollan nodded. "I suppose we'd best be on our way."

"Let's pray first."

Sylvia said a quick prayer for their safety and for justice to be served. As soon as she finished, she motioned to Hollan with her hand. "Lead the way. I'd like to get out of here before nightfall."

"Me, too." Hollan didn't need to be asked twice. She was in her least favorite place on the island. The swampy, marshy grounds were home to all sorts of creatures she didn't want to think about, let alone meet. She avoided the area like the plague in broad daylight, so being here after dark was a nightmare.

They didn't talk; they just made haste while walking through the scrub. Hollan pushed through far more spiderwebs than she wanted to think about. Her skin crawled as she wondered about the spiders that lived in the webs. The cooler weather might have chased them off, but she couldn't be sure.

She did a little jig as she walked.

Sylvia's soft laugh flowed through the evening air. "You're fine, Hollan. I see no spiders on your dress or hair." She knew about Hollan's fear of spiders, and she also knew how much Hollan hated this area.

The older woman clucked her tongue. "Love certainly is a mysterious thing."

"Pardon?" Hollan called over her shoulder, not slowing her pace.

"I know how you feel about this area. Yet you're willing to brave it for Jacob."

"I'm braving it in order to right the wrongs David has brought upon our families."

"How far do you plan to go?" Sylvia was out of breath. Hollan needed to slow her pace for the older woman.

"Not much farther. We're nearly at the end of the island now."

"And what are we doing here?"

Hollan stopped a few feet away. "We'll set up a bonfire." She moved her arms in an arc, gesturing toward the beach. The moon was climbing upward, reflecting off the water. Stars studded the sky. The only sound was that of the water lapping gently against the shore.

"Why here?" Sylvia frowned.

"We're at the bay end of the island. If any ships come

through here tonight, they'll be able to see where we are. Even better, the outlaws shouldn't be able to see us. We might not have use of the lighthouse, but we can warn the ships' captains of the island's danger from here."

"Good idea."

They busied themselves with gathering all the driftwood they could find.

"I want the fire to be big so it can be seen and so the outlaws can't easily put it out if they do see it."

"Another good idea."

They placed Spanish moss throughout the wood, and Hollan set it on fire. The fire flared, dimmed, and as she held her breath, flared again. Suddenly it caught and made its way through the pile of wood.

"It's magnificent!" Hollan trilled. "And the warmth feels wonderful against the night's chill."

"Indeed it does." Sylvia stared out over the darkened beach. "Only one problem comes to mind."

"What's that?" Hollan asked, turning to look at Sylvia with a smile. No problem could possibly dim her satisfaction now. She'd reached her goal to warn the sailors. Anyone drifting along the shore would see the bonfire and veer away from the land. Their main task had been accomplished.

"A large and very angry group of men seems to be headed our way."

Hollan looked up, and her heart leaped into her throat. Sylvia spoke the truth, and they didn't have time to hide. The men carried torches, and according to their well-defined silhouettes, they also carried very big guns.

❧

Jacob couldn't wait to get his hands on Hollan. He glanced at her father, wondering how the man had ever survived her. "I specifically told her to stay with Sylvia."

"Yes, you said to stay with Sylvia, which is exactly what she did." Gunter's forehead was creased with worry, but admiration for his daughter's spunk put a spark in his eyes. "In time, son, you'll learn to be more careful when choosing your words."

"I chose my words carefully this morning. Hollan deliberately chose to ignore them and twist them to her own benefit."

"Yes."

"Yes? That's all you have to say about it?" Jacob stomped along the path. The group of men walking with them tailed behind. They couldn't hear the conversation between Gunter and Jacob.

"You should know Hollan well enough by now to know she doesn't take well to direct commands."

"I'm her husband."

"And I'm her father. Apparently those two facts don't mean a lot to her when the time comes to make her decisions. Hollan has always acted first and thought later."

"We'll be changing that as soon as I have her safe."

Gunter's only response was an annoying chuckle. "We'll see about that, Jacob. The girl has a mind of her own."

Jacob sighed and pushed his hair back from his face. "I know. And I love her for it. I just don't like it when she puts herself in danger."

"God has His hand on you both. He won't fail Hollan—or us—now."

"You're right." Jacob sighed. "It's just that she makes me crazy with worry when she pulls a stunt like this. I want her home safe, knitting or sewing like a normal woman, but here she is ready to take on a band of roving privateers!"

"I would imagine that when Hollan continues to see her faith is safe with you, Jacob, she'll learn to settle down and let you lead."

"I certainly hope so, sir. I can't take much more of this."

"Meaning?" Gunter raised an eyebrow.

"Meaning, I want my wife safe at home."

"I understand. And I think we'll get her there tonight."

The sheriff walked up to join them. "Any idea what Hollan and Sylvia would have planned?"

"I know she was worried about the lighthouse not being lit. She wanted the seafarers to remain safe. She hated that the light was off during most of the war. She was also worried the men would destroy the cottage and everything in it."

They continued to work their way along the beach. The boats were pulled ashore just as they'd been the night before. It didn't seem as if Jonathon had been replaced by another guard.

Jacob glanced at Hollan's father. The man was pale but hanging in there. "Gunter, what do you think the chances are that David hasn't even missed Jonathon?"

"Pretty fair, I'd say, based on the fact that no one's been sent in his place."

They wove around the boats and continued along the shore, heading for the far end of the island.

The sheriff looked at Jacob again. "Which concern of your wife's would be the priority?"

"I think she'd worry first about the safety of others. My guess is she'll take care of the lighthouse situation first.'"

"Would she try to get into the lighthouse? Surely she'd know she'd be trapped inside as soon as the light was lit."

Jacob's heart dropped to his toes. What if his brother re-created the situation he'd been in with Hollan's mother? Jacob would throttle Hollan if she survived this! He'd never felt so much concern for another person. He couldn't lose her. Not now. Not after everything they'd been through. Not ever.

"You look ready to take on the outlaws single-handedly," Gunter observed.

"I feel like I could do just that. If they hurt Hollan..."

"She'll be fine, son. We're here now, and we'll find them. And although Hollan is contrary and impetuous, she's also very smart. She won't allow herself to be boxed into a corner."

"So how do you think she'll protect the lighthouse without endangering herself?" Jacob hoped with everything in him that Gunter was right.

"I believe—if I know my daughter—she'll set a bonfire on the beach."

"A bonfire, huh?" Sheriff Roberts rubbed his chin. "The fire would warn any captain of the island's dangers."

Jacob pointed ahead. "And it would lead my brother directly to Hollan's side."

❧

"What do we do now?" Hollan panicked. "My plan was that we'd set the fire and then move away the other direction. We'd go into hiding and make the next plan."

"I think we better figure out another plan and fast." Sylvia's voice was shaky.

They'd left their weapons in the trees. They couldn't get them now. In unison, they began to back away.

"We could always turn around and run for it."

Sylvia's laugh held no humor. "Yes, we'd run with a throng of angry men chasing after us with guns. We'd not likely get very far."

"Then we stand tall and go out fighting."

"I don't much like that plan, either. Don't you have anything else?"

"No. I have nothing."

The men were getting closer. Hollan reached over and took Sylvia's hand. Not the most heroic gesture, but she drew comfort from her friend's presence.

"We need to pray!" The urgency in Sylvia's voice sent a

chill down Hollan's spine.

Hollan heard Sylvia whisper a prayer for their safety. The words had no meaning in Hollan's terrified brain. She didn't want to be in David's custody again, especially now. He'd surely be angry about the ship going aground and about their escape.

The men continued to move closer.

"I'm starting to think we made a really bad decision in coming here."

The sneers on the men's faces scared Hollan to her toes.

"You're just starting to think that? I came to that conclusion when we first saw the throng of men coming our way."

The men neared the far side of the bonfire. Suddenly, as quickly as they'd appeared, they stopped and started to back away.

"Pray again, Sylvia, I think your prayers are working."

"I've already said my prayer, Hollan. I don't need to repeat myself to God."

The men looked wary and then alarmed. They turned heel and began to run.

"I don't understand."

"Me, either." Sylvia laughed. "But I like it!"

"I do, too." Hollan grinned with relief. "If and when we get out of this situation, let's not ever get ourselves into another."

A deep male voice whispered into Hollan's ear, "Is that a promise?"

Hollan screamed.

Jacob leaned around her. "Don't be afraid, Hollan. It's only me."

"You?" Hollan spun around. Her father, the sheriff, Uncle Edward—and most every man from town—formed a line that stretched across the beach.

"Papa." Her father grinned at her. He didn't seem too

angry. Jacob, on the other hand—he seemed angry enough for the both of them. He was possibly angry enough for the entire group.

"Well, I guess now we know why they turned and ran."

"Hollan. We'll discuss this later."

"That's all right," Hollan hedged. "We don't really have to discuss it at all. Let's just let bygones be bygones and start fresh like you said."

"We *will* discuss this." The fire reflected in his eyes and intensified the emerald green color. His golden hair hung loose in wild curls that danced across his shoulders. He towered over her, looking every bit the outlaw rogue she'd imagined him to be on their wedding day.

A commotion up ahead interrupted their conversation.

"What is it?" Hollan stood on her tiptoes but still couldn't see. Some of the men who had gone ahead returned.

"It seems the bonfire offered a much-needed diversion for the naval patrol. They were able to make landfall and sneak in behind David and his men. They're rounding them up as we speak."

A cheer rose up from Hollan's friends.

"But how—?"

The sheriff walked up with a huge grin on his face. "They knew where David was all along. They only needed the perfect break to come in and overwhelm them. Hollan, your bonfire created that diversion."

Hollan smirked at Jacob.

He quirked up the corner of his mouth and shrugged his shoulder.

Most of the men were drifting back the other direction. They were ready to head home.

Her father, Sylvia, and the sheriff walked ahead. Jacob and Hollan followed at a more leisurely pace.

"You know what this means." Jacob took Hollan's hand in his own.

"We can go home." Tears filled Hollan's eyes as she said the words. "Finally, after everything that's happened, we can go home."

"I like the sound of that, wife."

"That is, if we have a home left to go back to."

"Our cottage is tougher than a few crusty outlaws." Jacob smiled. "Our home will withstand more than that." He stopped and pulled her into his arms. "More importantly. . .home for me is wherever you are."

"Oh, Jacob, that's so sweet." Hollan considered his words. "But it's also very true. I feel the same exact way."

epilogue

Once again Hollan faced Jacob on a dune overlooking the ocean. This time nothing about the situation felt surreal. The wedding *was* the wedding of her dreams. And the man who stood beside her was as familiar to her as her own face. All of her loved ones stood alongside them to witness the event.

Their house—now put back in order after their adventure—and the untouched lighthouse stood sentry behind them. Samson ran between all the people, savoring their attention and happy to be back home.

The afternoon couldn't have been more perfect for their ceremony. The seagulls serenaded as they flew overhead. The ever-present sound of the waves crashing onshore brought a familiar comforting reassurance. Hollan would never tire of the roar of the surf from the Atlantic Ocean. She couldn't wait to wade along the tide line with her husband.

She turned her attention to the man at her side. She saw him clearly. She drank in his dimpled smile, his sparkling green eyes, and the way his golden hair blew in the wind. The sun silhouetted his broad shoulders and proved he wasn't the skinny boy who'd left three years before. The planes of Jacob's face had indeed changed with the years, but the changes were all for the better. And Hollan knew from recent experience that Jacob still didn't like to stay indoors any more than necessary, which accounted for his sun-kissed skin.

Her uncle's voice intruded on her musings. "Hollan. Jacob. I think we're all about ready. Let's do this ceremony right."

"We're ready, too," Jacob said with a grin. He gently squeezed Hollan's hand.

She nodded.

Uncle Edward smiled at her. "No regrets?"

"Never. Not a one."

"Jacob, has life on the island been everything you thought it would be?" Uncle Edward asked.

For a moment, Jacob could only laugh. Hollan watched him with a frown.

"Edward, we've been through a hurricane, I saved Hollan's life—more than once. I watched her captured at the hands of outlaws. I helped her escape. We slept outside with all the bugs on the Georgia coast and the various creepy-crawlies and reptiles. We found out about Fletcher's attack and were chased again by the outlaws. . . ."

"When you put it that way"—Hollan's heart plummeted— "I'm not even sure why you'd want to stay. Why *did* you keep coming for me, even when I put us in danger?"

"My unending love and protection of you is similar to God's unending love and sacrifice for us. Hollan, as long as God allows me the privilege, I'll be right here to pull you away from any danger that comes our way."

Hollan smiled.

"And Edward, to answer your question—" Jacob looked at them both, but his eyes settled on Hollan. The look of love he sent her filled her heart to bursting. "This experience has been everything I imagined and more."

"I'm glad to hear it, son." Uncle Edward slapped Jacob on the back and turned to welcome their guests.

Again he made quick work of the ceremony.

"Jacob, you may now kiss your bride."

Hollan grinned up at him. This was the perfect moment.

Jacob leaned forward and touched his lips to hers in the most gentle of kisses. Hollan's heart soared.

A Letter To Our Readers

Dear Reader:

In order that we might better contribute to your reading enjoyment, we would appreciate your taking a few minutes to respond to the following questions. We welcome your comments and read each form and letter we receive. When completed, please return to the following:

Fiction Editor
Heartsong Presents
PO Box 719
Uhrichsville, Ohio 44683

1. Did you enjoy reading *The Lightkeeper's Daughter* by Paige Winship Dooly?
   ❏ Very much! I would like to see more books by this author!
   ❏ Moderately. I would have enjoyed it more if

   _____

   _____

   _____

2. Are you a member of **Heartsong Presents**? ❏ Yes ❏ No
   If no, where did you purchase this book? _____

   _____

3. How would you rate, on a scale from 1 (poor) to 5 (superior), the cover design? _____

4. On a scale from 1 (poor) to 10 (superior), please rate the following elements.

   ____ Heroine   ____ Plot
   ____ Hero   ____ Inspirational theme
   ____ Setting   ____ Secondary characters

5. These characters were special because? _____
   _____
   _____

6. How has this book inspired your life? _____
   _____
   _____

7. What settings would you like to see covered in future
   Heartsong Presents books? _____
   _____
   _____

8. What are some inspirational themes you would like to see
   treated in future books? _____
   _____
   _____

9. Would you be interested in reading other **Heartsong
   Presents** titles? ❏ Yes ❏ No

10. Please check your age range:
    ❏ Under 18   ❏ 18-24
    ❏ 25-34   ❏ 35-45
    ❏ 46-55   ❏ Over 55

Name_____
Occupation _____
Address _____
City, State, Zip_____
E-mail _____

Wildflower Bride

Glowing Sun, born into the white man's world as Abby Lind, is one of few survivors after her Shoshone village is massacred. Forced to sever all ties to her adopted tribe, Abby wonders where she now belongs.

Historical, paperback, 320 pages, 5⅜" x 8"

_____

Heartsong

Presents

__HP803 *Quills and Promises*, A. Miller
__HP804 *Reckless Rogue*, M. Davis
__HP807 *The Greatest Find*, P. W. Dooly
__HP808 *The Long Road Home*, R. Druten
__HP811 *A New Joy*, S.P. Davis
__HP812 *Everlasting Promise*, R.K. Cecil
__HP815 *A Treasure Regained*, P. Griffin
__HP816 *Wild at Heart*, V. McDonough
__HP819 *Captive Dreams*, C. C. Putman
__HP820 *Carousel Dreams*, P. W. Dooly
__HP823 *Deceptive Promises*, A. Miller
__HP824 *Alias, Mary Smith*, R. Druten
__HP827 *Abiding Peace*, S. P. Davis
__HP828 *A Season for Grace*, T. Bateman
__HP831 *Outlaw Heart*, V. McDonough
__HP832 *Charity's Heart*, R. K. Cecil
__HP835 *A Treasure Revealed*, P. Griffin
__HP836 *A Love for Keeps*, J. L. Barton
__HP839 *Out of the Ashes*, R. Druten
__HP840 *The Petticoat Doctor*, P.W. Dooly
__HP843 *Copper and Candles*, A. Stockton
__HP844 *Aloha Love*, Y. Lehman
__HP847 *A Girl Like That*, F. Devine
__HP848 *Remembrance*, J. Spaeth
__HP851 *Straight for the Heart*, V. McDonough
__HP852 *A Love All Her Own*, J. L. Barton
__HP855 *Beacon of Love*, D. Franklin

__HP856 *A Promise Kept*, C. C. Putman
__HP859 *The Master's Match*, T. H. Murray
__HP860 *Under the Tulip Poplar*, D. Ashley & A. McCarver
__HP863 *All that Glitters*, L. Sowell
__HP864 *Picture Bride*, Y. Lehman
__HP867 *Hearts and Harvest*, A. Stockton
__HP868 *A Love to Cherish*, J. L. Barton
__HP871 *Once a Thief*, F. Devine
__HP872 *Kind-Hearted Woman*, J. Spaeth
__HP875 *The Bartered Bride*, E. Vetsch
__HP876 *A Promise Born*, C.C. Putman
__HP877 *A Still, Small Voice*, K. O'Brien
__HP878 *Opie's Challenge*, T. Fowler
__HP879 *A Bouquet for Iris*, D. Ashley & A. McCarver
__HP880 *The Glassblower*, L.A. Eakes
__HP883 *Patterns and Progress*, A. Stockton
__HP884 *Love From Ashes*, Y. Lehman
__HP887 *The Marriage Masquerade*, E. Vetsch
__HP888 *In Search of a Memory*, P. Griffin
__HP891 *Sugar and Spice*, F. Devine
__HP892 *The Mockingbird's Call*, D. Ashley and A. McCarver
__HP895 *The Ice Carnival*, J. Spaeth
__HP896 *A Promise Forged*, C.C. Putman
__HP899 *The Heiress*, L.A. Eakes
__HP900 *Clara and the Cowboy*, E. Vetsch

Great Inspirational Romance at a Great Price!

Heartsong Presents books are inspirational romances in contemporary and historical settings, designed to give you an enjoyable, spirit-lifting reading experience. You can choose wonderfully written titles from some of today's best authors like Wanda E. Brunstetter, Mary Connealy, Susan Page Davis, Cathy Marie Hake, Joyce Livingston, and many others.

When ordering quantities less than twelve, above titles are $2.97 each.
Not all titles may be available at time of order.